MISSISSIPPI
MEGALODON

Here's what readers from around the country are saying about Johnathan Rand's AMERICAN CHILLERS:

"I LOVE your books! They are AWESOME! You are my favorite author."
                                        -Michael M., age 9, Connecticut

"My favorite book so far is Poisonous Pythons Paralyze Pennsylvania. I like your books and hope to read more."
                                        -Jack A., age 8, Michigan

"Hey! If I write something cool about your books, will you put it in that blurb section you have in the front? Because your books really rock!"
                                        -Aarron J., age 10, Ohio

"I never used to like to read, and then I found your books. I've read every single one you've written. I can't stop!"
                                        -Whitney A., age 10, Montana

"I've read all your books, and they scare the daylights out of me!"
                                        -Logan L., age 7, Michigan

"Last summer, we drove to Michigan just so we could visit Chillermania! That place is cool!"
                                        -David L., age 10, Illinois

"My favorite book is Terrifying Toys of Tennessee. That book is terrifying, just like the title says!"
                                        -Allison H., age 13, Iowa

"YOUR BOOKS ARE AWESOME! I have already read 33 of your books and starting the 34th."
> *-Dante J., age 8, Pennsylvania*

"I just wanted to let you know that we read WICKED VELOCIRAPTORS OF WEST VIRGINIA in our class, and everyone loved it! I can't wait to read more of your books!"
> *-Corbin S., age 10, West Virginia*

"How come your books are the freakiest in the world? I've never read any other books like them. Keep writing!"
> *-Erik R., age 11, Delaware*

"I got one of your books for my birthday, and I loved it. Now, I can't stop reading them!"
> *-Samantha P., age 11, Michigan*

"I don't know if you know this, but everyone at our school is hooked on CHILLERS! They're the only books we read!"
> *-Marcus B., age 10, Ohio*

"You came to our school last year, and it was the BEST assembly we ever had! Please come back!"
> *-Tyler S., age 9, California*

"We had a contest at school to see who could read the most books written by you. I won! I've read every single book you've ever written. I love all of them! My favorite is WISCONSIN WEREWOLVES, because that's were I live. That book creeped me out really bad. It's great!"
> *-Addison S., age 12, Wisconsin*

"After reading DANGEROUS DOLLS OF DELAWARE, I had to sleep with the light on for two weeks. I can't believe how much that book freaked me out!"

-Rick A., age 11, Alabama

"I know your books aren't real, but when I'm reading them, it seems like they are. How do you do that?"

-Missy G., age 10, Oklahoma

"I love all of your books, but I have one suggestion: write faster!"

-Sean J., age 8, North Carolina

"When you write, do you wear those weird glasses? If you do, don't ever take them off, because your books are super awesome!"

-James T., age 10, Rhode Island

"I've read a lot of books, but yours are the best in the world! I think I've read all of them at least twice, and I read MUTANTS MAMMOTHS OF MONTANA three times! It's my all-time favorite book!"

-Melissa G, age 12, Michigan

"I got all three Adventure Club books for my birthday, and they're the best! Write more Adventure Club stories!"

-Namute H., age 11, Indiana

Got something cool to say about Johnathan Rand's books? Let us know, and we might publish it right here! Send your short blurb to:

Chiller Blurbs
281 Cool Blurbs Ave.
Topinabee, MI 49791

Other books by Johnathan Rand:

#25: Mississippi Megalodon

Johnathan Rand

An AudioCraft Publishing, Inc. book

Book storage and warehouses provided by Chillermania!©
Indian River, Michigan

Warehouse security provided by:
Lily Munster, Scooby-Boo, and Spooky Dude

American Chillers #25: Mississippi Megalodon
ISBN 13-digit: 978-1-893699-33-5

Librarians/Media Specialists:
PCIP/MARC records available **free of charge** at www.american-chillers.com

Cover illustration by Dwayne Harris
Cover layout and design by Sue Harring

Printed in USA

MISSISSIPPI MEGALODON

VISIT CHILLERMANIA!

WORLD HEADQUARTERS FOR BOOKS BY JOHNATHAN RAND!

Yooperland

Indian River

Alpena

Traverse City

MICHIGAN

Mt. Pleasant

Bay City

Grand Rapids

Lansing

Detroit

Kalamazoo

CHILLERMANIA!

I-75 Exit 313 then south 1 mile!

Visit the HOME for books by Johnathan Rand! Featuring books, hats, shirts, bookmarks and other cool stuff not available anywhere else in the world! Plus, watch the American Chillers website for news of special events and signings at *CHILLERMANIA!* with author Johnathan Rand! Located in northern lower Michigan, on I-75! Take exit 313 . . . then south 1 mile! For more info, call (231) 238-0338. And be afraid! Be veeeery afraaaaaaiiiid . . . .

1

Megalodon.

When I first saw the word, I didn't know what it meant. I didn't even know how to pronounce it.

Now, of course, I know *exactly* what a megalodon is. So do my friends, Tara and Landon. They know all too well what a megalodon is, and what it can do. They know, because they were with me. They saw it, too.

You see, a megalodon is a giant, prehistoric shark. At school last year, my teacher, Mrs. Biltmore, gave each of us a word to research. We had to find out what the word meant, and write a five page report. When she gave me the word *megalodon* on a small piece of paper, I looked at it and frowned.

"What's a mega . . . mega . . . however you say it?" I asked her.

Mrs. Biltmore smiled at me. "You'll have to find out yourself, Robbie," she said.

Great, I thought. I rolled my eyes and sighed. *Whatever it is, it's probably not something cool.* I was really jealous of some of my classmates who'd been given their assignments. One was given the word 'velociraptor,' which is a fierce, meat-eating dinosaur. In fact, I had just finished reading a book about velociraptors in West Virginia. It was a really freaky book. I wished I'd been given *that* word to research.

But when I found out what a megalodon actually was, I was really excited. Not only were megalodons giant, prehistoric sharks, but when they existed, they grew to over sixty feet long!

Once I started my research, I couldn't stop. Normally, I don't really like homework. But this assignment was super cool! I worked on my research paper for a couple of hours every night. Even on weekends.

The word *megalodon* means 'big tooth.' Megalodons are said to have lived millions of years ago and are believed to be the largest sharks that ever existed. Megalodons were so big that some scientists think they may have eaten huge whales!

I found more information about megalodons at the library and on the Internet, and even a few pictures of fossilized teeth, some of which are the size of a football.

Most scientists, however, say megalodons vanished a long, long time ago. But there are a few scientists and researchers who believe megalodons still exist today, in the deepest parts of the ocean.

Both groups of scientists are wrong. Megalodons *do* exist today . . . but not in the great depths of the ocean.

Megalodons—one of them, at least—lived in the dark, murky depths of Sardis Lake, Mississippi.

How do I know megalodons exist? I know this because Tara, Landon, and I came face-to-face with the gigantic beast one horrifying day last summer . . . .

2

One thing you should know about me: I love to fish. We have an old rowboat that Dad and I use to get around the lake. I've been fishing for nine years, ever since I was three. I love to fish more than anything else. We live in a house that's only a block from Sardis Lake, which is a huge, man-made lake in Mississippi. It's great for bass fishing. I've caught a couple of big ones. One of them weighed over five pounds!

Another thing you should know: I'm an excellent swimmer. I can hold my breath and stay under water for a full minute. Mom says I must be part fish, and I just laugh. That would be cool! I'd love to be part fish; then I could swim around and explore lakes and rivers and not have to come up for air.

But even though I'm a great swimmer, my mom and dad wouldn't let me take our rowboat out alone until I turned twelve years old and completed a boater safety course. Well, my twelfth birthday was last May fifteenth, and you can bet I took the course right away. It's easy to do, because you can take the course on-line. Two of my friends who live nearby—Tara and Landon Phillips—took the test, too. The three of us passed with flying colors, and as soon as we received our certificates, we made plans to take the rowboat out for a day of fishing.

"This is going to be so much fun, Robbie!" Tara said to me as we stood at the water's edge. We each carried our fishing poles, and I had my red tackle box that I got for my birthday. It contained dozens of lures and other things for fishing—spare line, some small tools, nail clippers—things like that. Tara carried the net, which we would use if we caught a big bass.

"Our very first trip together, just the three of us!" Landon said. "I hope we catch some big fish!"

"Even if we don't," I said, "we're still going to

have a great time. Come on . . . let's get our gear loaded into the boat."

Our dark green aluminum rowboat was tied to a dock. It's old, and a little beat up. Chunks of paint have been chipping off for a long time. Dad said he bought it before I was born, but it floats great and doesn't leak. It has a small electric motor mounted on the back. The motor doesn't make the boat go very fast, but it's quiet and doesn't scare the fish. Of course, the boat has two oars, and I'd use them if the motor's battery runs low, or if we want to be extra quiet.

The morning was cloudy and gray, and a little cool, too. It was late June, and Mississippi can get really hot during the summer months. This morning, however, the temperature hovered around sixty-five degrees, and it wasn't supposed to get too much warmer during the day. A thunderstorm had rolled through the night before, bringing colder temperatures and leaving an iron-colored sky and a hazy fog over the lake.

Which was fine with us. Some of the best bass fishing is on cloudy days. And we wouldn't have to worry about applying any sun screen. We had a cooler filled with sandwiches and snacks, so we wouldn't have to worry about going hungry. And Mom gave me her phone, just in case we had an emergency, so we wouldn't have to worry about contacting someone for help.

What we *would* have to worry about, however, was a fish.

Not a bass, bluegill, crappie, or other harmless freshwater fish, but an enormous monster that was lurking in the depths . . . watching and waiting.

3

"I hope the fish are biting today," Landon said as we walked along the old dock. The wood creaked beneath our feet, and the dock shifted and bounced under our weight.

"I hope so, too," I said. "It should be a good day, even if it's a little cold."

"There probably won't be many other people fishing, either," Tara said, "because it's cloudy and foggy."

I looked out over the lake. The water was dark, and a veil of thick, soupy fog hung heavy and low. I could actually feel it on my face, all cool and wet.

We loaded my tackle box, fishing poles, net, and cooler into the boat. I noticed that, because of the dark clouds above, the water beneath the dock was so dark I couldn't see the bottom. I knew the water was only about six feet deep, but it looked as black as night. It was eerie.

I stepped into the boat, picked up a yellow life vest, and tossed it to Landon on the dock. While he slipped into it and fastened the buckles, I tossed another one—a red life vest—to Tara. Problem was, my aim was a little off, and Tara had to lunge to the side to catch it.

Unfortunately, that was all it took. Her foot slipped off the edge of the dock, and she tumbled backward, flailing her arms wildly as she plunged into the dark water.

"Oh, no!" I said as I scrambled out of the boat and onto the dock. I felt terrible. It had been my fault that Tara had fallen. Mostly my fault, anyway.

I knelt at the edge of the dock, ready to reach down and help her back up. Nearby, the red life vest floated in the water . . . but there was no sign of Tara. She had vanished in the dark water. I wasn't worried, however, because Tara was a good swimmer. Still, I felt bad because she'd fallen in.

My eyes scanned the water, but I couldn't see her. With every passing second, I grew more and more worried. Landon did, too. We both knelt at the edge of the dock, worrying and waiting.

"Where did she go?" Landon asked. His voice trembled a tiny bit.

"Maybe she hurt herself and sank to the bottom!" I said.

Without another word, Landon slipped out of his life vest, dropped it to the dock, and jumped into the water. My heart was really pounding, and I wondered if I should use the phone Mom gave me to call for help.

She'll be okay, I told myself. *She'll have to go home and get into some dry clothing, but she'll be fine. She's a great swimmer.*

A movement far out in the lake caught my eye, and I turned. At first, I thought I was looking at a boat, because it was hard to see through the fog.

No, that's not a boat, I thought. *That's not a boat at all. That's a fin, and it's gigantic!*

In the next instant, the fin disappeared in the

fog.

What in the world was that? I wondered as I took turns glancing at the dark water below and out into the lake. It almost looked like a shark's fin . . . but that's impossible. Sharks don't live in fresh water. And besides: the fin was enormous. There is no shark in the world that could have a fin that big.

Suddenly, the water beneath me exploded, and Landon's head popped up. His eyes were wide. He looked frantic.

"She's gone!" he shouted in a panic. "I don't see her anywhere!"

My mind spun at light speed. I felt dizzy and really, really scared. I didn't know what had happened to Tara, but I knew we needed to get help, and fast.

I jammed my hand into my front pocket and yanked out the phone Mom gave me. My fingers were trembling as I punched in our home phone number.

Meanwhile, Landon had dived down again and vanished beneath the surface in a desperate search for Tara.

And what was that thing I saw way out in the lake? I wondered. There was no way—*no way*—it could have been a shark. Yet, that's what it had looked like: the fin of a giant shark.

No matter. I had other things to worry about, like—

What if it was *some kind of shark? What if it got Tara?*

I was about to punch in the last digit of our phone number when I heard a splash from behind me. I turned . . . and saw Tara. Her head had popped up a few feet on the other side of the rowboat, on the opposite side from where we had been looking for her. Her blonde hair stuck to the sides of her face, and she was smiling, and I now knew she had only been playing a joke.

Then, Landon popped up in front of me.

"I still can't find her!" he shrieked.

"She's over there," I said, pointing. "On the other side of the rowboat. She was only trying to scare us into thinking something had happened to her."

"Had you going, didn't I?" Tara called out as she began swimming, arm over arm, back to the dock.

"You totally freaked us out!" I said, holding up the small phone. "I almost called my mom and dad for help!"

"Yeah, well, you deserved it," Tara said. "If your aim with the life vest hadn't been so bad, I wouldn't have fallen in."

Landon reached the dock, and I helped him out of the water. Tara, too, reached the dock, and I grabbed both of her hands and pulled her up. The red life vest I'd tossed was floating next to the rowboat, and I reached down and plucked it out of the water.

"This is just great," Landon said angrily. Water dripped from his drenched clothing. He spread his arms wide. "Now, we're *both* soaked."

"Oh, quit being a crybaby," Tara said. "It's just a little water. It's not going to kill you. Let's go home and get changed."

Tara was right. A little bit of water wasn't going to hurt us. It was the gigantic beast lurking *in* the water that we would have to worry about—and we'd be seeing *that* creature soon enough.

5

While Landon and Tara went home to change their clothes, I picked up my fishing pole and made a few casts into the lake. Last year, I caught a nice-sized bass while fishing from the dock.

All the while, I thought about the strange thing I'd seen far out in the lake. Of course, it was foggy, and I didn't get a good look at it. But it looked like a fin, although I knew that was impossible. It *must* have been a boat. Or my imagination. Maybe I just *thought* I saw something.

Whatever it was, I didn't see it again. And

although I made a few dozen casts while waiting for Landon and Tara, I didn't catch any fish.

Fifteen minutes later, Landon and Tara came back wearing fresh, dry clothing.

"Try to stay out of the water this time," Landon said to his sister as they walked along the dock.

I had already put on my life vest, and I handed one to Landon and one to Tara.

"You guys ready?" I asked.

"We are now," Landon said.

I knelt down and held the boat steady while Tara and Landon got in and sat. Then, I untied the two lines securing it to the dock and got in myself. I sat in the back, near the motor, and Landon sat in the middle. Tara was seated at the front.

There was about an inch of rain water in the bottom of the boat, left there by the overnight storm. I picked up a large red coffee can and handed it to Landon.

"Bail out the water," I said, "and I'll get us on our way."

Landon began scooping up water and dumping it over the side of the boat. I pressed the start button on the electric motor, and it instantly hummed to life.

The boat began to move forward slowly.

"The lake looks creepy with all this fog," Tara said as the boat slipped through the water.

"I think it looks sort of cool," Landon said as he scooped up some water with the coffee can and dumped it over the side of the boat. "It looks like the beginning of a scary movie."

We had no idea how right Landon would turn out to be.

6

"Where are we headed?" Tara asked.

"I thought we'd try fishing in the shallows near Timberlake Campground," I replied. Last year, my dad and I caught a bunch of big bass at a spot not too far from shore. It was a great place to fish, and not many people knew about it.

Landon finished bailing the rain water out of the boat and set the coffee can at his feet. "My uncle said he caught a six pound bass last week," he said. "Wouldn't it be great to catch one that big?"

"I bet a fish that big would put up quite a fight,"

I replied. "I bet he had a hard time getting him into the net."

"What kind of lures are we going to use?" Tara asked.

"I'm going to use a rubber crayfish," I said. "That's what I caught my last big fish with."

"Not me," Landon said. "I'm going to use a big spinner." He held it up to show me. The spinner was about three inches long, with a treble hook at the bottom. A treble hook is actually three fish hooks joined by a single eye. There was a teardrop-shaped piece of metal hooked to it. You used the spinner by casting it out, letting it sink a couple of feet, then reeling it in slowly. The teardrop spun around as it was pulled through the water. They work pretty well, depending on what the fish are biting on that particular day.

"Try a surface lure," I told Tara. "Something that makes some movement on the top of the water. Out of the three different lures we'll use, one of them has to work."

"Do you have one I can borrow?" she asked.

I opened up my tackle box and pawed through the plastic trays until I found a red and white lure with two treble hooks.

"Try this one," I said, and I handed it to Landon to pass to Tara. "Careful of the hooks."

By then, I'd forgotten about the strange, fin-like object I'd seen farther out in the lake. I'd convinced myself it must have been another boat, and I never thought about it again. I was too excited to get started fishing.

"Doesn't this boat go any faster?" Landon asked.

I shook my head. "It's only an electric motor, so it doesn't go very fast. I keep telling Dad to get one of those gas-powered outboards, but he says we don't need it. He says they make too much noise."

"It just seems like we're going awfully slow," he said.

"Don't worry," I replied. "We should be there in just a few minutes. There's—"

I was distracted by a motion out of the corner of my eye, and I turned.

If horror was a truck, I would have been run over. Landon gasped, and Tara shrieked. They, too, were seeing the same, unbelievable thing I was seeing: the fin of what could only be from a giant shark.

And the thing was heading in our direction!

7

Landon freaked out, leaning to the side and nearly causing the boat to capsize. Tara screamed.

Me? All I could do was stare, wide-mouthed, as the enormous fin came closer and closer, cutting through the gray fog. There was nothing we could do, and nowhere we could go. With only the tiny electric motor, I was sure there was no way we'd be able to outrun the creature.

"It's a giant shark!" Landon shrieked. "Get this thing moving! We have to get out of here!"

I turned the throttle to increase our speed, but

our boat was already going as fast at the motor would allow. So, I grabbed the oars that were resting inside the boat, dropped them into the water and began rowing like mad. It didn't help. I just couldn't row fast enough.

The fin kept coming faster and faster, and showed no signs of slowing.

This can't be happening! my mind screamed. *Giant sharks don't exist, and they certainly don't exist in Sardis Lake!*

The fin was still coming toward us, but I noticed it was getting smaller as it sank into the dark water.

"He's diving down!" I shouted. "But he's probably not going away!"

"This is horrible!" Tara shrieked. "I don't want to be eaten by a giant shark! I'm not even thirteen!"

The fin vanished, but I knew if my calculation was right, the shark would be right beneath our boat. I looked into the water, but it was too dark, and I didn't see anything. The only thing I could see was the choppy reflection of myself and the reflection of the gray fog.

"Let's get out of here!" Landon cried. "We've got to get off the water before that thing gets us!"

But now we had another problem. The fog had gotten thicker, and we could no longer see the shore. All around and above us, the only thing we could see was the dark surface of the lake and the curtain of misty, gray fog.

"I don't know which way to go," I said as my eyes scanned the dark waters for any sign of the shark. "It's too foggy."

"I think the dock is that way," Landon said, pointing.

Tara shook her head and pointed in the opposite direction. "I think it's over there," she said.

"I'm calling Mom," I said, and I reached into my pocket and pulled out the phone she gave me. However, at that very moment, Landon made a quick movement with his arm.

"Let's head over there," he said, snapping his arm out. His movement was fast, and he didn't see the small phone in my hand. His finger ran straight into my wrist, knocking the phone from my palm. I tried to catch it, but it was too late. The phone bounced once on the edge of the rowboat and plopped into the water, where it quickly vanished beneath the waves.

"Nice going," I snarled.

"I didn't mean to do that," he said. "I'm sorry. Your mom is going to be really mad at me."

"I'm not worried about Robbie's mom," Tara said. "I'll worry about her later. I'm more worried about that thing we just saw."

This wasn't good. We were lost in the fog, we'd lost our only way of contacting help, and worst of all: there was a giant shark lurking in the depths, probably watching us at that very moment.

I thought things were about as bad as they could get . . . but I was wrong. They were going to get a worse.

A *lot* worse.

8

We were silent for a few moments as we contemplated our situation. The only sound was the hum of the electric motor and the waves slapping gently against the aluminum rowboat.

A megalodon, I thought. *That's what that thing was. That's the same creature I had researched for my classroom assignment.*

But megalodons existed millions of years ago, and they lived in the ocean, in salt water. Sardis Lake is *fresh* water. Sharks shouldn't be able to live in fresh water.

But this one did. We'd seen it with our own eyes. There was no mistaking the giant fin for anything else.

A megalodon.

"I know what that thing is," I said to Landon and Tara. I told them all about my research and my report.

"I didn't think sharks lived in fresh water," Landon said.

"They're not supposed to," I replied, shaking my head. "I've never heard of such a thing."

"Yeah, well, I know what I saw," Tara said. "That thing was a shark, or a megalodon, or whatever it is you called it. And if we don't get off the water, he's going to gobble us up."

"But we have no way of knowing which way we're heading," I said. "We might be going farther and farther into the lake at this very moment. In fact, that thing could be following behind us, hidden under water, at this very moment. He could be watching us right now."

"We can't just drift around out here," Landon said, scanning the surface warily.

"Actually," I said as I shut off the electric motor,

"that's exactly what we *should* do. We're going to sit right here and be still and quiet. When the fog lifts, we'll be able to see where we need to go. Besides: if we don't do anything to attract the attention of the megalodon, maybe he'll go away. It's a big lake. Let's hope he goes far away."

"We don't even know for sure what it is," Landon said. "All we saw was a fin. Just because you *think* it's a megalodon doesn't mean it *is* one."

Landon was right, of course. But two seconds later, something happened that would remove all doubts as to what the creature was.

9

Tara was the first to notice it. When she spoke, her voice was barely a whisper.

"Hey," she began, "I know this sounds weird . . . but does anyone feel that?"

"Feel *what*?" I asked.

"Shhhhh," she said. "Listen."

All I could hear were the hollow sounds of waves gently licking at the aluminum boat.

But then, I *did* sense something. A feeling. It was very strange. It was a feeling like something was about to happen. Something serious. It didn't feel like anything or anyone was watching us. It felt more like a premonition—like something was coming, or something was about to happen.

Suddenly, about one hundred feet away, the water exploded with such force that it sounded like a bomb going off. As it happened, the three of us were looking in that very direction, and we all watched as an enormous, giant shark—bigger than a school bus—came all the way out of the water. He leapt into the air the way a bass does when he's trying to throw a hook from his mouth.

But a bass is only a few pounds. The thing we saw must've weighed fifty tons, and when the beast plunged back into the lake, it sent a huge shower of water fifty feet into the air.

We were so freaked out that we couldn't say a word. We couldn't gasp, we couldn't scream. All we could do was stare out over the lake where we'd seen the giant shark.

Finally, Tara spoke.

"That . . . that thing is humongous!" she said.

"It's impossible," I said. "Like I said: those things can't live in fresh water."

"Hey," Landon said. His voice was trembling.

"We all saw the same thing. That was a giant shark, or a megalodon, or whatever. We have to get off the water, fast!"

"We're never going to outrun that thing," I said. "The best thing we can do is just stay quiet. If we don't make a lot of commotion on the surface, he might leave us alone."

"Wait a minute," Tara said. Her voice trembled, and she sounded scared. "We have something else to worry about."

"What?" Landon asked.

Before Tara even had a chance to reply, I knew what she was talking about. When the megalodon came crashing back down into the water, it created an enormous, raging wave . . . a wave that would be upon us in seconds!

"Hang on!" I shrieked. *"The wave is going to capsize the boat!"*

10

The wave grew in size as it rolled toward us, until we were looking up at a rising mountain of water. The only thing we could do was hold on to our seats and wait for it to hit.

"Hang on tight!" I shouted again.

The swell reached the boat, and we started to turn. I could feel us rising up into the air, sliding sideways, and the boat began to roll.

"Lean into the wave!" I shouted.

Our boat was a tiny speck of dust compared to the size of the wave, and it lifted us up into the air and rolled beneath us. Then, we were plunged back down as it went by. The sheer force had nearly caused the boat to flip over, but, by some miracle, we hadn't.

Unfortunately, it was enough to jar the electric motor, which broke loose . . . and fell into the lake. I tried to grab it before it sank, but I was too late. The battery cable snapped, and the motor vanished in the dark water, just like the phone had. The large, rectangular battery was still in the boat, but it wasn't going to do us any good without the motor.

"I can't believe we didn't flip over or get knocked out of the boat," Landon said. "That wave was ten feet tall!"

"But we lost the motor," I said. "My dad is going to be really, really mad. And Mom will be, too, since we lost her phone."

"Let's not worry about your dad being mad," Tara said. "Like I said before: let's worry about getting off the lake alive."

Tara had a good point. In the scheme of things, having Dad get mad at me for losing the motor wasn't a big deal. Besides: it really wasn't our fault. Once Dad found out *how* it was lost, I was sure he would understand. He and Mom would just be happy the

48

three of us were alive.

If, of course, we still *were* alive. At that moment, I wasn't so sure we would ever make it off the lake without being eaten by that thing. I had no idea where the megalodon came from, or if there were more. I didn't know if it would come after us. All I knew about them was they were the most vicious fish to have ever lived, and they ate everything in their path. In fact, the three of us probably wouldn't amount to more than a snack for such a gigantic creature.

"I vote we start rowing," Tara said.

"Me, too," Landon said. "We can't just sit here while that thing is around. He's probably watching us right now."

I looked around. The fog still hadn't lifted. If anything, it had become thicker.

But then, I heard something.

A car horn.

Most importantly, I could tell the direction from which it came.

"All right," I said, "I'll row. That car horn came from over there." I pointed, then reached for the oars. "It didn't sound like it was too far away. We can't be more than a few hundred yards from shore."

I turned around in my seat, so I could row by drawing the oars toward me.

"Keep an eye out for that thing," I said. "I'll watch behind us, and you guys watch the front and the sides."

"How fast can you row?" Tara asked.

"Not as fast as a megalodon can swim, I'm afraid," I replied.

We can make it, I told myself. *We can make it to shore, and then we can call the police or something. People have to be warned to stay out of the water.*

I dipped the oars into the lake. While I rowed, I watched the dark water behind us, scanning the surface nervously. The fog seemed thicker than ever.

Five minutes later, I was thinking we were going to make it.

"Tara, can you see the shore, yet?" I asked.

"Not yet," Tara replied. "But we can't be far."

I turned my head, but I couldn't see any sign of land. All I could see was fog, and it made our situation seem all that much worse. On a sunny day, Sardis Lake is a happy place, full of boats and other small water craft. The thick fog made the lake seem cold and lonely. Haunting, even.

I turned and looked back behind us . . . and that's when I saw something emerging in the gray haze.

A giant fin was slicing through the fog, following us!

11

"*Here he comes!*" I shouted. "*He's following us!*"

The fin rose into the sky. It was big—taller than an adult—and as it came closer, it seemed even bigger, slashing through the gray fog and the dark water like a giant knife.

"*Row faster!*" Landon shrieked.

I began rowing like crazy. The muscles in my back, shoulders, and arms burned. The oars splashed water as I rowed, propelling the boat as fast as I could make it go.

Still, the fin came even closer. Faster.

Finally, I became exhausted, and I stopped rowing and slumped forward in defeat.

"What's the matter?!?!" Tara shouted.

I shook my head. "I can't row any more," I replied.

"I will!" Landon shouted. *"Move over!"*

"Wait," I said, pointing. "Look! The megalodon is turning away!"

Behind us, we watched the fin as it turned. It was about fifty feet from us, which meant the shark's head was a lot closer.

But the creature had turned and was now circling the boat.

"Let's not move," I said, gasping for breath. "He went away before. Maybe he will again."

I was so scared that my entire body was trembling. My heart pounded and my jaw quivered. A billion questions spun through my head, but the most important one kept surfacing every few seconds: *are we going to make it off the lake alive?*

The megalodon circled us once, twice, three times. In the thick fog, it was all that more eerie-looking. Not being able to see the shore or the sky made me feel even more frightened and alone.

It took nearly a full minute for the shark to complete a wide circle around the boat. During this time, none of us spoke or moved. We were too horrified.

Then, the fin began to sink into the water. We watched it get lower and lower, smaller and smaller, until it finally vanished beneath the surface.

"It worked," Tara said with a sigh of relief. "He went away."

"But he's still around," I said. "The best thing we can do is just sit here and wait. If I keep rowing, it's just going to attract his attention again. Sooner or later, someone will come looking for us. We just have to be patient."

"If we wait any longer, we're going to get eaten," Landon said. "Did you see how big that thing was when it leapt out of the water? That thing could eat us and the boat in one gulp!"

"We don't have any other choice," I said. "If we just stay here and don't make any noise or commotion, the megalodon might not pay any more attention to us. It worked just a few minutes ago. When I stopped rowing, he went away."

So, that's what we did. We simply sat in the

boat, looking around, gazing into the fog, watching and waiting. It was an awful feeling. Not only were we really scared, but we were also helpless. If the megalodon wanted us for his next meal, there was nothing we could do about it. There was no way we would be able to defend ourselves.

The more time that went by without seeing any sign of the megalodon, the better I felt. Sardis Lake is big, and the humongous shark might be a long way away by now. I hoped he was, anyway.

He's gone, I told myself. *We'll just sit tight, and we'll be okay. When I'm not home on time, Mom will call. When I don't answer the phone she gave me, they'll come looking for us. They might even call the police. All we have to do is wait.*

I was sitting in the rowboat, telling myself this, when I heard a different sound nearby.

A popping sound.

And another.

A bunch more.

"Look!" Tara said, and her arm shot out. I turned to see what she was pointing at.

Not far from the boat, large bubbles were rising to the surface. The bubbling became frantic, and soon a huge area of water was churning and boiling. Then, we saw something moving just beneath the surface.

Something *huge.*

The megalodon was surfacing only a few feet from our boat!

12

"Start rowing!" Landon shrieked. "We've got to get away from that thing!"

"There's no way I can row fast enough!" I screamed back. Still, I grabbed the oars and pulled, moving away from the patch of rising bubbles.

As I rowed away, we watched as the water continued to boil. I was sure the creature was attacking, and it was the end of the line for all three of us.

Suddenly, the head of the megalodon broke the surface . . . but it wasn't a giant shark, after all.

It was a submarine!

As if things weren't already crazy enough! First, we see a giant shark in Sardis Lake . . . and now, we happen upon a submarine!

Crazy.

I stopped rowing and stared at the strange sight before us. Only one part of the submarine came out of the water, but there was no mistaking what it was. The part that broke the surface was barrel-shaped, dark gray, and made of steel . . . and it was only twenty feet away from our boat.

Tara shook her head. "No one is going to believe any of this," she said, "and I've already pinched myself, so I know I'm not dreaming."

I grabbed the oars and rowed away from the sub, since I wasn't sure what was going to happen next.

"Do you think anyone's inside?" Landon asked.

"I would think so," I said. "Someone has to be operating it."

We waited and watched, but nothing happened. We were also on the lookout for the megalodon, but we saw no sign of him. The only thing we could see was the submarine and the heavy curtain of gray fog.

Tara began to speak. "Well, maybe—"

A metallic noise from the sub caused her to pause. Then, the submarine hatch opened up. We saw a single hand, then another.

Suddenly, a woman appeared! All we could see were her neck and head. She had shoulder-length red hair and wore wire-rimmed glasses.

"Don't just sit there in the water!" she said. Her arm appeared, and she motioned us toward her. "You're lucky you haven't been eaten alive! Hurry up and get in here!"

"Who are you?" I asked.

"I'll explain later," the woman said. "I've been following the megalodon, and I saw your boat. I'm glad I found you in time. All three of you are lucky to be alive. Now hurry!"

I was still a little nervous. I had no idea who the woman was.

But, on the other hand, she was right: we'd been really fortunate so far, considering the fact that there was a giant shark in the water. We would probably be a lot safer in the submarine than we would be in our rowboat, and I decided to do what the woman asked.

"Let's go," I said to Tara and Landon. "The lady is right: we'll be safe in the submarine. I'll row us over."

My decision came too late. Just as I grabbed the oars and started to row, we were suddenly, explosively propelled upward. It was such a quick, violent movement that it felt as if we had been shot out of a cannon or as if a bomb had gone off beneath us. We were sent flying out of the rowboat, tumbling high into the air. And when I looked down, all I could see was a gigantic gray snout and an enormous, open mouth filled with razor-sharp, foot-long teeth.

I heard Tara and Landon scream. Then, I heard someone else scream . . . and it took me a moment to realize it was me. But it didn't take me long to realize something else: it was the end of the line for the three of us. Our luck had run out, and we were about to become shark food.

13

I splashed down into the water and plunged beneath the surface. Instantly, I popped back up, buoyed by my life vest. I sputtered and spit lake water from my mouth.

Suddenly, the rowboat slammed to the water two feet away, upside down. If it had landed any closer, it would have hit me. My tackle box fell into the water, and so did the cooler and the net. One of the fishing poles hit me in the shoulder.

I was disoriented for a moment, unsure of what had happened or why. Then, I saw the submarine. The woman was frantically waving at me, urging me to swim over.

And boy, did I *ever!* I swam faster than I ever had in my life. The shark had vanished beneath the surface, and I couldn't see his fin, but I knew he was close by. Every horrifying second, I kept thinking he would attack, opening up his powerful jaws to swallow me whole.

Nearby, Tara and Landon were also swimming toward the sub. Water splashed as the three of us tried to make it to safety before the creature attacked again.

Landon made it to the sub first. By now, the woman had climbed out of the hatch and was kneeling on a small, metal deck that was only a few inches from the water's surface. She reached out, grabbed Landon's hand, and pulled him up and out of the water.

Tara was next. The woman helped her up and out.

I was still swimming like mad when the three of them—the woman, Tara, and Landon—all started yelling.

I stopped swimming and turned to look behind me . . . only to see the blade of the shark's fin!

"You can make it!" the woman shouted. *"Keep swimming!"*

I kicked with my legs and crawled through the water with my arms with all the strength I had. It was hard, too, because my arms, back, and shoulders were already tired from rowing so much.

"Come on!" the woman shouted.

"Hurry!" Tara shrieked.

I wasn't going to take the time to turn and see how close the megalodon was. All that would do was slow me down. Instead, I stayed focused, forging ahead, kicking and swimming, in a desperate attempt to make it to the submarine. Although I'm a good swimmer, I was really glad I had on my life vest, because it helped me stay on the surface.

It was a horrifying feeling, knowing that, at any moment, I might feel the megalodon's sharp teeth, knowing that I might be swallowed in a single, quick gulp. As I swam toward the sub, seconds seemed like hours. It felt like it was taking forever to make it to the vessel, but, when I finally did, I didn't waste any time getting out of the water. I reached up, and the woman grabbed both of my hands and pulled me from the lake.

"Climb inside the sub!" she ordered. "Go down the hatch!"

Behind me, the huge fin was still coming toward us. Not far away, the rowboat floated upside down, partially sunk. My red tackle box floated nearby, but there was no sign of the net, the cooler, or the fishing poles.

Tara was first down the hatch, followed by Landon, then me. I climbed up and in, only to find a ladder sinking into the depths of the sub. I scrambled to it and began my descent carefully, as the metal rungs were slippery against my wet hands and shoes.

Above me, the woman crawled in. She closed the hatch with a loud clang. Our surroundings grew dark, but there was a light glowing below.

I continued my descent. In six more steps down the ladder, I reached the floor. Tara and Landon were standing nearby, dripping wet. I took a step back to let the woman continue down the ladder.

All of a sudden, we heard a deafening pound. A light flickered a couple of times. The submarine lurched violently, sending the three of us to the floor. The woman, however, was still holding the ladder, and she didn't fall.

"I think we made him a bit angry," the woman said. "He's not happy that you got away."

The submarine was stable again, and she helped us to our feet.

"What in the world is going on?" I said. "Where did that thing come from? Where did *you* come from?"

"I'll tell you in a moment," she replied. "First, follow me."

The woman walked past us and down a narrow corridor. As the three of us followed, I looked around. There were long, metal pipes crisscrossing all over the place. The walls, floor, and ceiling appeared to be solid steel. There were only a few small lights, and everything seemed cold and dark and lonely. I read somewhere that some people spend months in military submarines without ever surfacing. Months! If I had to stay in such a confined area for that long, I think I'd go crazy.

We followed the woman as she made her way through the submarine. The ceiling was low, and she had to duck a number of times, so she wouldn't hit a pipe or a bar. Tara, Landon, and I didn't have to duck at all. We weren't that tall, so it was easy for us to make our way through the ship.

"We're dripping water all over the place," I said to her.

"That's fine," the woman replied. "A little water isn't going to hurt anything."

The woman stopped and motioned to her left. There was a doorway, of sorts, except, instead of being in a rectangular shape like most doors, this one was oblong, and we would have to duck down and step up to get through.

"Watch your step," she said as she bent low and climbed through the portal. Landon followed, then

Tara, then me.

The room we entered was a bit more spacious, about the size of our living room. There were all kinds of blinking lights, hums, and computer monitors. Most of the screens were dark, but one of them showed what appeared to be the surface of the lake, as I could see the dark water, fog, and what looked like our capsized rowboat not far away.

Directly in front was a large, round window, and we could see directly into the lake. I could see the shimmering surface above and the blue-gray water beneath. It was like looking into an aquarium, without the fish and coral and plastic plants and seaweed.

"I'm going to submerge," the woman said. "Then, I'll explain to you what I know."

We remained silent while she went around the room, flicking switches, pressing buttons, turning dials, and pecking away at the numerous computer keyboards. She moved swiftly and without hesitation.

And the strange thing was that we were submerging, going deeper and deeper into the lake, but it didn't feel like we were moving at all. In fact, the only way I knew we were moving was by looking through the giant window in front of us. I watched as the surface above drew farther and farther away. As we descended deeper and deeper into the depths, the light from the surface faded. Soon, the window was completely dark, and none of the computer screens showed anything, either.

Finally, the woman stopped her work. She came over to where we were standing.

"I'm sorry I don't have any chairs for you to sit," she said. "I'm afraid I don't have luxuries like that in this submarine."

"I don't need to sit down," I said as I slipped my life vest off, and Tara and Landon did the same. Water continued to drip from my drenched clothing. "I just want to know what's going on."

The woman looked at each of us, then began to speak. What she told us was *incredible*.

15

"First of all," she began, "my name is Jennifer Monroe, and I'm a marine biologist."

Landon frowned. "What's that?" he asked.

"Basically," Jennifer replied, "I study undersea life. I've been doing this for twenty years. But for the past year, I've devoted most of my time to finding what most people believe doesn't exist in Sardis Lake: a megalodon."

"You don't have to convince us," I said. "We know better."

Jennifer nodded. "Over the years, there have

been reports of a giant creature in Sardis Lake. Some even reported that they'd seen a shark. They weren't taken seriously, because sharks don't live in fresh water.

"But last year, a man found this." Jennifer turned and strode to a wall where there were several metal cabinets. She opened one, pulled out a shoe box, and raised the lid.

"Look," she said, lowering the box, so we could see its contents.

Inside was a long, sharp, grayish-white tooth, triangular shaped, shiny and smooth. It was over twelve inches long.

"That's a shark tooth!" Tara exclaimed.

Jennifer nodded. "To be precise, it's the tooth of a megalodon. It was found by a man on the other side of the lake."

"But that tooth could be millions of years old," I said. "It's not proof that a megalodon lives in Sardis Lake."

Jennifer shook her head. "Carbon dating showed that this tooth isn't old at all," she said. "In fact, it was estimated to be only three or four years old."

"But how could a megalodon live in Sardis Lake without being discovered?" Landon asked.

"That's what I'm trying to find out," Jennifer replied. "I've been searching for the creature for a year. I've been unsuccessful . . . until yesterday. That's when I recorded this."

Jennifer moved to a computer keyboard. On the wall, a screen flashed to life. The recording showed what appeared to be a bright light at the bottom of the lake. The atmosphere was murky and thick, and there were clumps of dark green weeds and a few small logs. Other than that, there wasn't anything to see. Not even a fish.

"I don't see anything," Tara said.

"Watch closely," Jennifer replied.

We watched the large screen, but still saw nothing.

"Just a second," Jennifer said in an excited whisper. "Keep watching."

Slowly, we could make out a dark form in the depths. The image was fuzzy because whatever was making the shadow was farther away. But as it came closer, into the light, there was no mistaking what it was: an enormous shark.

A megalodon.

Jennifer was beaming. "Finally!" she said as she adjusted her glasses with her index finger. "Proof! I recorded the megalodon yesterday afternoon. It was the first time I've found it in Sardis Lake, and I've been searching since last summer."

I couldn't take my eyes off the image on the screen. The megalodon was massive—whale-sized—and it turned and began to swim slowly away, out of the light. Then, it vanished in the hazy darkness.

"This is unbelievable," I said. "Where did that thing come from?"

"I have a theory," Jennifer said.

"What's a 'theory?'" Landon asked.

"A theory is like an idea," Jennifer explained, "or a hunch, based on the evidence and information gathered. I've been studying the possibility of megalodons living in fresh water for a long time. Most scientists say it's impossible. However, from what I've found out, I think it's not only possible, but probable. And now that we've discovered an actual, living megalodon, we know the truth."

"But shouldn't we get out of here?" Tara asked. "I mean . . . that thing tried to eat us. He attacked our boat and your submarine."

"The sub is on autopilot, and we're headed for the docks at my laboratory. You can call your parents from there, and they can pick you up."

"Don't you have a radio in this thing?" Tara asked.

"I did," Jennifer replied, "but it's old. It quit working a month ago. I've been meaning to get it fixed, but I've been too excited about finding the megalodon to do anything else."

"But what's your theory?" I asked. "How is it that a megalodon is alive today, living in Sardis Lake?"

"I believe that—"

Suddenly, the submarine rocked violently to the side, shaking the entire ship. The lights went out, and we were knocked to the floor.

Jennifer had said we were safe, as long as we were in the sub.

She was wrong.

16

Somewhere, a siren screamed. We were in total darkness, and the sound seemed like it was coming from all around us.

"Is everyone okay?!?!" Jennifer shouted above the siren.

"I'm all right," I said.

"Me too," said Landon.

"I'm okay," Tara said.

"Stay right where you are," Jennifer ordered. "I'll get the emergency lights on."

In the darkness, I could hear Jennifer moving.

Then, the only thing I could hear was the siren.

And I was scared. I didn't know what had happened. Maybe we'd run into something.

Maybe something had run into *us*.

"I have a really bad feeling about this," Tara said. The lights hadn't come on yet, but it sounded like she was only a few feet from me.

"We'll be all right," I said, but I wasn't sure if I believed it myself. Still, just saying it made me feel a little better. It's always best to look on the bright side. That's what my dad always says, anyway.

After a few moments, a couple of dim, yellow lights came on. The siren fell silent. On the other side of the control room, Jennifer stood with her back to us, tapping at a computer keyboard.

"There's some damage to the sub, but we're okay," she said. "But we're going to have to surface so I can repair a few things." I scrambled to my feet, and Tara and Landon followed. We walked across the control room to where Jennifer was standing.

"What happened?" I asked.

"I'm not sure," she said. "I don't understand it."

"Don't understand what?" Tara asked.

"The megalodon attacking the sub," Jennifer

replied. "I didn't think he would do that."

She continued tapping at the keyboard. "First things first," she said. "Let's see what we've got."

Suddenly, a bright light from outside the submarine lit up the large portal in front of us.

We were at the bottom of the lake!

I could see dark patches of seaweed and sand. There were several large clumps of what looked like decaying vegetation. I tried to look up and see the surface, but we were too deep.

Then, we saw something else, and this time, it wasn't a recording being played back on a computer.

This time, it was real, and happening right before our very eyes . . . .

17

The megalodon cruised in front of the submarine. He moved slowly, taking his time. He approached the sub, and, even with his mouth closed, his razor sharp teeth protruded out. I could see his eyes, and I knew he was looking at us. He could see us through the glass portal, and I knew what must have been going through his mind.

There's a few tasty human snacks in that big steel can, he was thinking. *All I gotta do is get it open.*

A chill rocked through my body. Seeing such a massive, horrifying creature so close made my blood turn cold. At school, we went to the zoo for a field trip, where they had an aquarium filled with sharks. It was really cool, but the sharks were only five or six feet long. They would look like tiny minnows compared to the beast before us!

"He's . . . he's watching us," Tara stammered. "He can see us in here."

"I don't think he can," Jennifer said. "The spotlight on the outside of the sub is very bright, and the light in here is faint. I think there's too much glare for him to actually see inside. But, just to be safe, stay very still. Don't move an inch."

I don't think I could have moved if I tried. I was too scared. It felt like every muscle in my body had turned to stone.

After about a minute, the megalodon moved away. He swam off to the right of the submarine and vanished into the gloomy depths.

"Did he attack the submarine?" I asked. "Is that what happened?"

Jennifer shook her head. "I don't know," she replied. "He might have just been curious and nudged us. After all, he doesn't know what a submarine really is. He might think the sub is another megalodon, like him."

"Maybe he's looking for a girlfriend," Landon said.

Jennifer turned. "You might be right," she said. "Right now, it's impossible to know what the creature is thinking."

Oh, we'd know soon enough. We were about to find out the megalodon wasn't looking for a girlfriend.

The truth was, he was *mad*. Maybe he thought the submarine was another megalodon invading his territory. For whatever reason, he was furious with the sub, and he was out to destroy it . . . with us inside!

18

After a few minutes of working at her computer keyboard, more lights came on. Somewhere, an engine chugged and hummed to life. My clothing was still wet, but at least I wasn't cold, as it was quite warm in the submarine.

"There," she said. "Now we can ascend to the surface and make repairs. It shouldn't take too long. We're not very far from the docking station at my laboratory. You'll be able to call your parents and be on your way home soon."

Jennifer walked to the front of the submarine and stood at what looked like the helm. It was a tall desk with lots of electronics and switches and dials. I had no idea what they were for.

"Is that where you control the sub?" Landon asked.

"Yes," Jennifer replied. "Mostly, it's controlled by computers, but someone must program them. And now that the submarine is damaged, I'll have to pay close attention to everything."

"You started to tell us about your theory," I said, "right before that thing hit us."

"Yes," Jennifer said. "It's only a theory, but I believe this megalodon, as a baby, was frozen in amber millions of years ago."

"You mean tree sap?" I asked. I'd seen bugs frozen in amber before. But I'd never heard of anything else trapped in amber. Certainly not a fish.

Jennifer nodded. "A few years ago, a large piece of amber was found about a mile from the lake. It was the size of a washtub, and it contained several small fish frozen within it."

"Sharks?" Landon asked.

Jennifer shook her head. "Not sharks, but they

were a species of saltwater fish that became extinct long ago. I believe that's how our megalodon came into existence. I believe that, somehow, it became frozen in amber, which perfectly preserved the creature. For millions of years, the creature was in a dormant state, still alive, in the amber. It was as if he was sleeping.

"In the late 1930s," Jennifer continued, "when the Sardis Dam was being built, I think the workers unearthed the giant slab of amber, but didn't know it. The dam opened in 1940, and water flowed in from the Talahatchie River. Over the years, the water softened the amber, and it decayed, freeing the baby megalodon, and—"

"—and the water somehow revived the megalodon," I interjected.

Jennifer nodded. "Exactly. The water brought the shark back to life, and, although it wasn't salt water, it had been frozen in amber so long that the fish adapted and survived. For years, it's been in Sardis Lake. Some people claim to have seen it, but the very idea of a megalodon existing in this day and age seems ridiculous. Nobody took any of these sightings seriously."

"They'll have to, now," Tara said.

I frowned. "But if the megalodon has been here all this time, how come it hasn't eaten anyone?"

Jennifer shook her head. "I'm not sure. The only thing I can think of is that, for the most part, animals—including fish—try to stay away from humans. Sure, there are shark attacks in the ocean, but humans aren't on the top of a shark's list of food. In fact, I think the megalodon in this lake primarily eats other freshwater fish. There are lots of fish in the lake, which would contribute to his enormous size. The other possibility is that the megalodon might be able to go back into periods of semi-hibernation for years. That seems like the most likely possibility. He could remain unnoticed for years, resting at the bottom of the lake."

"Look!" Tara suddenly said, pointing to the large glass portal in front of us. "It's getting light out!"

I looked out the window, and up. Above us the darkness was fading into a gauzy gray color. The sub was approaching the surface.

But then, we saw something else . . . and the four of us soon realized that we weren't going to make it.

19

The massive megalodon appeared once again. He kept his distance, and all we could see was his cloudy form, but we could tell he was watching us as we made our ascent.

While we watched, however, the giant shark approached. This time, he went over top of us, causing Jennifer to stop our ascent. She turned the submarine, and we continued to rise, but the megalodon came toward the ship once again, forcing us to change course.

"It's like he's playing with us," Jennifer said as

we watched the enormous creature through the glass portal.

Once again, I was both amazed and terrified of its massive size. It was fascinating to see such a creature, but I would much rather have been watching a television show or reading about it in a book. Being so up close and personal with a real, live megalodon was something I would have never imagined . . . or wanted.

"Do you think that thing has eaten anyone?" Landon asked.

Jennifer shook her head. "While it's certainly possible, I don't think he has. We would have heard about someone missing in the lake. I don't think he's hurt anyone, yet."

Yet.

I didn't like that word. Here we were in a submarine in Sardis Lake, face-to-face with the largest, fiercest prehistoric fish in the world that hasn't eaten anyone . . . yet.

Yet.

It wasn't a comforting thought.

The megalodon vanished into the murky depths. Oh, he was still around, I was sure, watching us from the shadows. But we could no longer see him.

"He damaged the oxygen processor when he hit the submarine," Jennifer said. "It's not serious, and it will take me only a few minutes to repair. But we've got to be surfaced to do it."

With the giant shark no longer in sight, Jennifer continued piloting the submarine upward. We could see the surface twenty feet above us. Still, there was no sign of the megalodon.

"Just a few more feet," Jennifer said.

"Maybe the thing swam away," Tara said.

"It's possible," Jennifer said. "He might have become bored or went to look elsewhere for food."

"The lake is so big, he could go anywhere," Landon said. "I hate to think about all the people swimming at beaches."

"Actually, the people swimming at beaches wouldn't have anything to worry about," Jennifer said. "The water is too shallow for the megalodon. However, people in boats or small watercraft could be in danger. Still, for whatever reason, I don't think the megalodon has attacked anyone."

"Except us," I reminded her.

"That's true," Jennifer said. "Maybe his tastes

are changing."

Finally, we reached the surface. It was kind of cool, being that the portal window remained under water. We could look out and up and see the waterline and the surface. Below that, Sardis Lake faded into a soupy, thick darkness.

Jennifer tapped at her computer keyboard, made a few adjustments on some equipment, and flipped a couple of switches. It sure looked like she knew what she was doing.

"There," she said. "We're stabilized. You guys wait here, and I'll be right back."

"We're not going anywhere," Tara said.

She spoke too soon.

Suddenly, the submarine was rocked by another pounding shudder. This one was much harder than the last one had been, and it sent all four of us flying across the control room. I slammed into something and fell to the floor. The submarine lurched to the side, and the power went out.

What was worse, when I looked out the glass portal, I could see the surface was getting farther and farther away. I felt an odd sensation, like being on an elevator that was dropping way too fast.

"We're sinking!" Landon shrieked.

Landon was right. We were going down . . . and we were going down *fast,* headed for the bottom of Sardis Lake.

20

It was worse than a nightmare. I could feel us plummeting to the depths, dropping like a rock tossed into the lake. The only light came from the portal window, and as we sank farther and farther from the surface, our surroundings within the sub grew darker and darker. In seconds, there was no light at all. The only thing I could hear was the sound of bubbles blipping and blooping.

"Everybody hang on to something!" Jennifer shouted in the darkness.

I had already grabbed ahold of something—a

pipe, I think—that ran along a wall. I grabbed it and pulled myself to my feet. Holding the pipe with both hands, I was able to keep steady. Thankfully, although the submarine was in a free fall, we were descending evenly. Things would have been a lot worse if we were tumbling end-over-end and rolling around.

"Everybody just hang on," Jennifer repeated. "We're not sinking fast enough to do much damage when we hit bottom."

As soon as she said those words, the submarine came to an abrupt, solid halt. The whole vessel shook, and I heard eerie, metal creaks and groans as the ship settled on the lake bottom.

"Is everyone all right?" Jennifer asked.

"Yeah," I replied.

"I am," Tara said.

"I bumped my knee," Landon said. "But it doesn't hurt very bad."

I'm not afraid to admit: I was more scared than I have ever been in my life. We were in total darkness at the bottom of Sardis Lake. Not only that, there was a giant megalodon lurking in the waters. He was probably watching the submarine at that very moment.

I heard some shuffling nearby.

"Everyone hang tight for a minute," Jennifer said. "I'll see if I can get the emergency lights on again."

She brushed past me in the darkness.

"Are we going to get out of here alive?" Tara asked quietly.

"Yes, we will," Jennifer answered confidently. "This submarine is pretty solid. It's going to take a bit more than some bumps and dings to make any serious damage. And if the megalodon gets really serious, I have a way of taking care of him."

"Looks like he's pretty serious right now," Landon said. "He's seriously trying to make us his next meal."

In the darkness, I could hear Jennifer on the other side of the control room. I heard switches being flicked and buttons being pressed, but nothing happened. All the while, Tara, Landon, and I said nothing. All we could do was wait and hope that Jennifer was right, that the submarine would be fine.

Of course, we'd still have to deal with the megalodon, but right now, that wasn't our biggest worry. Our biggest worry was getting the submarine to work, so we could get back to the surface and head for the dock at Jennifer's laboratory.

I was still sitting on the floor when suddenly, I felt something cold against my leg.

And *wet.* Of course, my clothing was still wet from when the megalodon had knocked us out of the boat, but the water I now felt against my skin was cold.

"Hey," Tara said. She, too, had noticed the water. "My arm is wet. There's water in here!"

Now, we had another horrible thing to worry about: *the submarine was leaking!*

21

Things couldn't get much worse.

I got to my feet as more water entered the control room. It sloshed beneath my sneakers, and I knew it would only be a matter of time before it rose over my ankles.

Suddenly, light bloomed. It was thin and faint, as if only half-lit. There was water all over the floor, but I had no idea where it was coming from.

"I've got the auxiliary power working," Jennifer said. She was standing at the helm, squinting in concern as she looked at a computer screen.

"But what about the water?" Landon asked. His voice quaked and trembled. He was scared. We all were.

"I'm turning on the emergency pumps," Jennifer said. "We're taking on water, but it's not coming in very fast. The emergency pumps should filter it back into the lake."

"Is there anything we can do?" I asked. I felt so helpless, not being able to do anything. Of course, I didn't know anything about submarines, and I wasn't sure what I could do.

"Not now," Jennifer said as she hurried around the control room. "I've got to get these computers back on line, so we can get moving again. The important thing is this: don't panic." She stood in front of a computer keyboard mounted on a shelf on the wall near the glass portal. "We're going to get out of here," she continued. "Just keep your cool. If I need any help, I'll let you know."

I looked at Tara, and she looked at me. She had a look of sheer terror in her eyes. Last year, a chipmunk got trapped in a garbage can in our garage. I don't know how he got there, but he sure looked scared. He was shaking and his dark eyes brimmed with total fear. I felt really bad for him. I slowly tilted the garbage can to the side, and he scampered off and vanished.

That's the kind of terror Tara was feeling, and I was just as afraid as she was. Landon looked at me, and he, too, had an expression of fear and bewilderment.

And I wondered what my mom and dad were doing at that very moment. They were probably working around the house, outdoors. They certainly had no clue where we were or what we were up against.

What if we don't make it out of the sub? I wondered. *What if the megalodon attacks again? What if I never see Mom or Dad again? What if—*

I mentally shook the thought away. *Stop thinking like that, Robbie,* I told myself. *Like Dad always says: look on the bright side.*

Well, it was hard to find the bright side of our current situation. But we were all alive, and we were all okay. Jennifer got the power working, and the computers were coming back up. We'd sprung a leak somewhere in the sub, but the pump was pushing the water back into the lake. Maybe we would make it, after all.

"Why isn't this working?" Jennifer said loudly. She sounded frustrated, and she began tapping furiously at the computer keyboard.

"What's not working?" I asked.

Jennifer didn't answer. She just kept tapping away at the computer. She was working furiously, and her fingers were flying. Her eyes never left the computer monitor before her. She squinted and looked very concerned.

Landon reached up and rubbed his throat. "It's getting hard to breathe," he said. "I'm trying to take a deep breath, but I can't."

"I noticed the same thing," Tara said. She, too, gently rubbed her throat.

I hadn't noticed it before, but now that Landon mentioned it, he was right: it *was* getting harder to breathe.

"The oxygen processor has completely shut down," Jennifer said. "That's how we get air to breathe in the sub. If the oxygen processor quit working . . . ."

She didn't finish her sentence, but it wasn't necessary. We all knew what she meant. We knew what was happening.

We were at the bottom of Sardis Lake in a crippled submarine . . . and we were running out of air.

22

"Okay," Jennifer said while she continued tapping at the computer keyboard. "The important thing is to stay calm. We need to save every bit of air we can. The more we move around, the more our muscles work, and the more oxygen they need. Stay calm, and we'll make it out of this."

Suddenly, I heard the thick sound of a motor starting somewhere in the submarine. The entire vessel seemed to vibrate.

"Yes!" Jennifer said. "I've got it! All the power is back on!"

She backed away from the keyboard and returned to the helm, where she quickly flipped some switches and began tapping away at the keyboard on the desk. We heard squeaks and squeals as the sub began to move. I could feel the vessel slowly begin to rise.

"We're on our way to the surface," Jennifer said. "You guys doing okay?"

"Yeah," I said, even though it was getting harder and harder to breathe.

"I'm fine," Tara said.

"Me, too," Landon replied. "But I hope we make it to the surface soon."

"What happens if you can't get the oxygen thingy fixed?" Tara asked.

"I will," Jennifer said. "I can fix it."

"I'm not worried about that," I said. "I'm worried about the megalodon."

Jennifer turned and looked at us. She had a smile on her face. "I wouldn't worry about him," she said. "I have a secret weapon. I didn't want to have to use it, but I'm afraid we might have to."

She flipped a switch, and the glass portal at the front of the control room lit up. She'd turned on the lights on the outside of the submarine. There wasn't much to see except murky water.

"One of you, come up here to the front," she said.

I was closest, so I walked to where she was standing.

Jennifer pointed to what appeared to be a single joystick or some sort of game controller. It was built into a desk next to her. There was a large button to the left of it, also built into the desk.

"Grab the controller in your right hand," she said.

I did as she asked.

"There's a power switch to the right of the controller," Jennifer said. "Turn it on."

Again, I did as she asked. When I flipped the switch, a movement in the glass portal window caught my attention. At first, I thought it was the megalodon, but it wasn't.

A large plus sign—rifle crosshairs—appeared in the glass.

"Move the controller around and see what happens," Jennifer said.

When I did, the crosshairs moved. It was like

aiming for a target, just like many of the video and computer games I'd played!

"What is this thing?" I asked.

"It's a stun torpedo cannon," Jennifer replied. "You aim by moving the controller around. When you have the target in the crosshairs, press the button on the left. There is a barrel mounted above, outside the submarine, that fires the stun torpedoes."

"This thing shoots torpedoes?" I asked.

"Actually," Jennifer replied, "the torpedoes are just bursts of high energy light. It should be strong enough to stun the megalodon and stop him from coming at us."

"I've never heard of such a thing," Tara said from behind me.

"It's an experimental device created by a friend of mine who works at a marine laboratory in Florida," Jennifer explained. "It's designed to keep potentially dangerous marine life—sharks, killer whales, barracuda, things like that—away from humans without harming them or other aquatic life. I'd hoped I wouldn't have to use it, but I think we'll have to, especially if that thing attacks us again."

"Have you ever used it before?" Landon asked.

He had walked over to where I stood, along with Tara. Both were looking at the controller in my hand and the crosshairs in the glass portal. I moved the joystick around, and the crosshairs in the portal window responded by moving back and forth, just like a video game.

"I've never had a reason to," Jennifer said.

"So you don't know if it'll work or not?" Tara asked.

Jennifer's smile faded. "No," she said. "I don't. But I think it will."

We'd find out, all right—a lot sooner than any of us would have thought.

23

Gradually, as we approached the surface, our surroundings beyond the submarine grew lighter. The water became a deep, dark green that slowly grew lighter and lighter, finally turning more blue as we neared the surface. I was glad we were no longer at the bottom of the lake, but going up and down, up and down was beginning to make me feel like we were trapped in a giant, steel yo-yo.

"Be ready to fire if you see the megalodon," Jennifer said. "Do you have the hang of it?"

"I think so," I said. "It's not much different from

a video game."

"No, it's not," she agreed. "Actually, it's even easier to use. Just be ready."

Tara spoke. "But what if the thing comes up from behind us?" she asked.

Jennifer frowned. "I'm afraid there'll be nothing we can do, then," she said with a sigh. "I'm sorry you guys got mixed up in this. But you're better off here, in the submarine, than you were on the lake."

"You're not kidding," Tara said. "If you hadn't come along, we would have been shark snacks."

Then, I had a crazy thought. Once in a while, that happens. I'll be thinking about something, when, all of a sudden, I'll get an entirely different idea. I was gripping the stun torpedo controller in my right hand and looking out the glass portal for any sign of the megalodon, and all of a sudden, I thought about school starting in the fall.

Just think how cool it would be if my teacher asked everyone in our class to write about what they did on their summer vacation! I would have the best story of all!

Of course, that's assuming we'd get out of Sardis Lake with our lives. At that moment, I wasn't too sure.

Jennifer, however, seemed confident, and I was glad. She was a smart lady, and she kept her cool during the tough times we were having. She was looking on the bright side . . . and I was trying to, as well.

"There's the surface," Jennifer said. We all leaned forward and peered out the glass portal, looking up. We could see the surface looming above, and our surroundings continued to brighten.

As focused as we were on the surface, none of us noticed the dark shape coming up from the depths until it was too late. In one moment, we saw the movement in the shadows beneath us. In the next moment, the giant megalodon slammed nose-first . . . straight into the glass portal.

24

Once again, the submarine was rocked by another impact, and Tara, Landon, and I were tossed violently to the floor. Jennifer, however, remained on her feet, and she fought to stay in control of the sub. Thankfully, the power hadn't gone out again. And by some miracle, the glass portal hadn't shattered. That would have been a disaster, as it would have meant the end for us for sure. Water would have poured inside, and there would have been no way to stop it. We would have sunk to the bottom of the lake, and then—

I didn't want to think about what would happen next.

I leapt to my feet and grabbed the stun torpedo controller. Jennifer had already steadied the sub, and I was ready to fire . . . but the megalodon wasn't in sight.

"He surprised us again," Jennifer said as Tara and Landon got to their feet.

"I'm ready, now," I said, scanning the waters through the glass portal.

Suddenly, I saw the megalodon. He was quite a ways away, and I could only see his dark silhouette. I maneuvered the controller until the crosshairs in the glass window were on his shadow—and pressed the button.

I guess I was expecting some sort of explosion, like a shotgun blast or something, but it wasn't like that at all. There was a dull thud that wasn't very loud. Through the portal, I saw a yellowish, tube-like missile above the sub, heading toward its target. Bubbles trailed behind the torpedo, rising to the surface in shiny, swirling, silver clusters. The missile wasn't moving very fast, either, which surprised me. But then again, I didn't know very much about how the stun torpedo worked.

We held our breaths as the tube-shaped bundle of energy sliced through the murky water. Unfortunately, the megalodon had moved on. He was no longer in the area I had targeted, and the stun torpedo passed by harmlessly. Then, it vanished in the depths.

"He's going to have to be closer before you shoot," Jennifer said. "But maybe you won't have to. I'm going to get to work fixing the oxygen processor. When I open up the hatch, fresh air will come in, so it'll be easier to breathe. Keep your eye out for the megalodon."

That was good news. My lungs were beginning to hurt from gulping for air, and now I noticed my skin had broken a sweat. It would be good to have some fresh air to breathe.

Jennifer tapped away at the computer keyboard, and the rumbling of engines stopped.

"I'm headed up," she said. "Keep an eye out for the shark." She hustled through the control room and vanished down the corridor.

"Can you believe this is happening?" Tara asked. "I mean . . . I thought we were just going fishing. I thought the worst part of our day was when I fell off the dock."

"We're fishing, all right," I said. "But it's a whole different kind of fishing."

"You're both wrong," Landon said. "That thing is doing the fishing. That megalodon is fishing . . . for us."

A couple of minutes went by, and we said nothing more. We just stared out the glass portal, watching for any sign of movement.

"Hey," Tara finally said. "It's getting easier to breathe."

She was right. And the air smelled sweeter, fresher, and not as stale. That alone was enough to lift our spirits.

Jennifer returned to the control room.

"Good news and bad news," she said.

"What's the bad news?" I asked.

"The bad news is that the oxygen processor is badly damaged. I wasn't able to fix it, which means we can no longer submerge. We'll have to remain on the surface."

"What's the good news?" Tara asked.

"The good news is that we're not far from my

laboratory dock. I'm going to head us in that direction, and we should be there soon. Have you seen any sign of the megalodon?"

We shook our heads. "No," I replied.

"Well, I'm sure he's still around," Jennifer said. "Let's just hope we've seen the last of his attacks."

Things were looking up, but we weren't out of danger, yet. We still had to make it to Jennifer's laboratory dock . . . and we quickly found out it wasn't going to be all that easy.

25

The clean, fresh air felt great, and breathing was a lot easier, now that the hatch was open. Sure, the hatch was on the other side of the sub, and we were still in the control room, but we could feel the difference in our lungs. The air was circulating throughout the vessel, and it wasn't a struggle to take a breath.

"It's still a little foggy outside," Jennifer said, "but we can navigate back to my laboratory dock with the submarine's computers."

"And I'll man the stun torpedo controller," I said.

Jennifer looked at Tara and Landon. "I need you two to do something, too," she said.

"I'll do anything if it'll get us out of the water faster," Landon said.

"Me, too," Tara echoed.

"If the megalodon attacks," Jennifer continued, "he can attack from any angle. We can only see what's in front of us. If he comes at us from behind or the sides, we won't know it. You two go up to the hatch. Don't go onto the deck—stay in the sub. Just poke your heads out and look around. If the megadolon is near the surface and *does* come toward us, you'll be able to see his fin. If you do, it'll be important to know which direction he's coming from. That way, I can maneuver the sub in that direction, and Robbie will have a chance to get him with the stun torpedo before he hits us again."

"Let's hope we don't see him anymore," Tara said.

"There's a good chance we will," Jennifer said. "Something tells me he's not going away."

Tara and Landon strode off and made their way through the submarine. I could hear them talking to one another as they headed toward the ladder that led up to the main hatch.

They hadn't been gone more than a minute, when they started screaming.

"There he is!" Landon shouted. His voice echoed and bounced around in the submarine. *"He's directly behind us!"*

Immediately, Jennifer began changing our course. The sub began to turn, but it moved slowly.

"How far away is he?" I shouted.

"He's still a little ways away!" Tara shouted. *"But he's heading in our direction!"*

The submarine continued to turn.

"There!" Jennifer pointed to the glass portal. "Can you see him?"

"Yes," I said, gripping the controller in my right hand. My palm was slippery with sweat as I moved the controller and guided the crosshairs to my target.

"Wait until he gets closer," Jennifer said. "Don't shoot until I say so."

We watched as the distant form in the murky waters came closer and closer, getting bigger and bigger. Soon, I could make out its v-shaped nose.

"Now?" I asked.

"Not yet," Jennifer said.

The megalodon was still coming at us and showed no signs of turning away. His mouth was open, and I could see upper and lower rows of enormous, triangular-shaped teeth . . . and that's where I placed the crosshairs. If my aim was good, the stun torpedo would go right into his mouth. I wasn't sure what that would do to him, but Jennifer had said it wouldn't kill him—it would just stun him and stop him from attacking.

"Get ready," Jennifer said.

"I am," I said. My right hand was shaking on the controller, and my left was trembling on the button. I held the crosshairs in place, keeping them on the open mouth of the attacking megalodon.

I sure hope this works, I thought. *If it doesn't, we're in a lot of trouble.*

"Now!" Jennifer said.

I aimed . . . and fired.

26

When I pressed the button, there was a dull thud as the stun torpedo was launched. The yellow tube of energy came into view through the portal window, heading right for the attacking megalodon. Again, the torpedo left a trail of shimmering, swirling bubbles that rose to the surface.

The giant fish showed no sign of turning away. For a moment, it seemed I was watching a television show or a movie. What was happening couldn't be real, not here and now, and certainly not in Sardis Lake.

But as the gargantuan beast continued coming toward the submarine, I was forced to realize that, indeed, I wasn't watching television. What was happening was real . . . and so was the danger. As he came closer, I could see his eyes burning with a dark fury, and it seemed he was looking right at me. His mouth was still open, and his enormous, long teeth seemed more menacing than ever. I hated to think what would happen if one of us was caught in his jaws.

The barrel-shaped stun torpedo sped toward the megalodon's gaping, hungry mouth. The fish was still coming right at us, and if the stun torpedo missed, we were going to be in trouble.

The giant shark kept coming, but it spotted the stun torpedo. The creature suddenly dove down, and the stun torpedo and its harmless trail of bubbles went above him.

"I missed again!" I cried in despair.

"Everyone hang on!" Jennifer shouted. "Just in case he—"

She wasn't able to finish her sentence. Without warning, the submarine was jolted so suddenly and violently that I was thrown over the desk and onto the floor. Even Jennifer was knocked off her feet. On the other side of the sub, from the hatch, I heard Tara and Landon screaming, along with some banging and a loud thud.

I hit the floor hard, but I wasn't hurt. I scrambled to my feet.

"Tara! Landon!" I shouted. "Are you guys all right?!?!"

"We're okay!" Tara shouted. Her voice echoed through the sub, and it sounded dull and hollow. "That thing sure hit us hard!"

I looked out the portal. The only things I could see were the murky, blue-gray waters and the silvery surface of Sardis Lake a few feet above. The only thing I could hear was the low drone of the submarine's engines.

It took a moment to realize something else was wrong, and when I looked to see where Jennifer was, I was horrified to see she still hadn't gotten to her feet. In fact, she was on the floor . . . and she wasn't moving.

I raced to her and knelt down. *"Jennifer!"* I exclaimed, reaching down and shaking her shoulder. *"Jennifer! Are you all right?"*

Jennifer didn't move, even when I shook her

gently.

Tara appeared in the main cabin, followed by Landon.

"What's the matter?" Tara asked.

"It's Jennifer," I said solemnly. "I . . . I think she's dead!"

27

Tara and Landon walked to where Jennifer lay on the floor. Tara knelt down and put her ear close to Tara's mouth.

"I can hear her breathing," she said. "She's not dead. Maybe she hit her head and got knocked out."

"It doesn't look like she's bleeding," Landon said.

"Jennifer?" I said again, as I gently shook her shoulder. She didn't respond.

We were really in trouble, now. Not only did we face the danger posed by the megalodon, but the only person who knew how to pilot the submarine was unconscious.

Suddenly, the massive form of the giant shark filled the large portal. He was so close that his body blocked out everything else.

Then, he stopped. His giant dark eye was only inches from the glass portal, and he glared at us. Looking at that eye, I felt fear like I had never known before. The things I had been afraid of: bee stings, falling off my bike, failing a math test . . . those things all seemed so silly, now. If there was one thing I saw in the eye of the megalodon, it was this: fearlessness. He was not afraid of us. He knew he was the king in this lake, and he was going to make sure we knew it.

Slowly, he swam off. Oh, he wasn't going very far, I was sure of that. He had just moved away, waiting for his next opportunity to strike.

Then, Jennifer stirred. Her arm moved, and her head shifted a little bit.

"Jennifer?" I asked. "Are you okay? Can you hear me?"

Jennifer groaned and slowly rolled over. She had a large, swollen lump on her forehead from where she'd hit something. It was turning red and purple.

"What . . . what happened?" she stammered as she rubbed her eyes with her hands. She winced when she touched the welt on her head.

"That thing attacked us again," Landon said.

"Yeah," I said. "Really hard, too. It knocked all of us off our feet. You must have hit something when you fell."

"This is really serious," Jennifer said. "I didn't think the megalodon would be that powerful. And I certainly didn't expect him to attack us so forcefully."

She made a motion to stand, and Landon and I grabbed her arms and helped her up. She was still a little wobbly, but she looked like she was going to be okay. Still, Landon and I held her arms, just to make sure she could keep herself steady.

"Thanks," she said. "Are you guys all right?"

"We're fine," Tara said. "But that thing really wants us bad."

"There's no time to waste," Jennifer said. "I'll get us moving toward shore again." She looked at Tara and Landon. "Can you two still be our lookouts?" she asked.

Tara and Landon nodded.

"Yeah," Tara said. "We just have to hold on

131

tighter."

"I'll man the torpedo cannon," I said.

"Let's move," Jennifer said urgently, and she went to the helm of the submarine to take control.

I was glad she wasn't hurt badly. Sure, she had a nasty lump on her head. But it could have been a lot more serious. Last year, a friend of mine from school was riding his bike without his helmet. He fell and hit his head, and he had to go to the hospital. The injury to his head was very serious. He had to have a bunch of stitches, and he stayed in the hospital for over a week. He's fine now, and he still rides his bike . . . but he always wears his helmet.

The submarine's engines grew louder, and I could feel the sub starting to move. Tara and Landon left the control room and headed for the main hatch. As for me, I returned to my position at the desk and grasped the joystick, ready for action. I sure hoped that if I had to use the stun cannon again, my aim would be better.

"Do you see anything?" Jennifer hollered to Landon and Tara.

There was a pause, and then Tara answered from the main hatch.

"No," she said. "It's still pretty foggy."

"Can you see land?" Jennifer yelled.

"Just a little bit," Landon replied, his voice echoing through the sub.

"That's good news," Jennifer said to me. "We're not far from docking. Just a few more minutes, and we'll be safe."

One minute ticked past, then two. Then three.

We're going to make it, I thought. *We're going to get off the lake, and we'll be safe. This nightmare will be over.*

I was actually getting a little excited. I couldn't wait to tell Mom and Dad and all my other friends about what we saw and experienced. We might even be on television! That would be cool!

All the while, my eyes never left the glass viewing portal in front of me. I scanned the murky waters, looking for any sign of the megalodon. The only things I saw were a few other fish, including a large bass that I would have loved to catch.

But that would be for another day. Our rowboat had capsized and was floating somewhere in the lake. Hopefully, if we found it, it wouldn't be too damaged. Of course, I don't think anyone was going to set foot in

Sardis Lake—not until they got rid of the man-eating megalodon.

Tara's excited voice suddenly echoed through the submarine. "Hey! A boat is coming toward us! And it's a big one!"

A boat! I thought. *Maybe someone knows we're in trouble, and they're coming to help!*

Things were looking up . . . until the submarine was once again rocked by another violent crash. I was able to hold onto the desk and not fall. Jennifer had a firm grip on the submarine's controls, and she, too, managed to stay on her feet.

But in our control room, the disaster was unfolding. The megalodon had attacked from beneath us and smashed his huge snout into the front viewing portal. Glass shattered, and water flooded in so fast that, in mere seconds, it was up to my ankles.

"To the hatch!" Jennifer said. *"The sub is going down! We'll have to abandon ship!"*

"Abandon ship?!?!" I exclaimed as I frantically got up from the desk. "But that *thing* is out there!"

"We don't have any other choice!" she replied. *"Go! Go!"*

There's an expression I'd heard when things like

this happen: *out of the frying pan, into the fire.*

Basically, it meant that, no matter what, your goose was cooked.

And for us, it would mean that we were about to become shark biscuits . . . and there was nothing we could do about it.

28

I sprinted as fast as I could through the submarine, but I couldn't move very fast, given the tight surroundings. I had to be careful not to bang my head into anything. Jennifer was right behind me. I could hear the roar of the engines, but the sound was being drowned out by the thundering of water gushing into the control room.

We reached the ladder. I grabbed the steel rungs and scrambled up like a frantic squirrel.

"What's going on?!?!" Landon asked.

"The megalodon smashed the glass portal!" I replied as I climbed. "Water is coming in, and the sub is going to sink! We have to abandon ship!"

As I reached the open hatch and looked out, I could already see that the submarine was sinking lower in the water. Water was about to begin pouring in the hatch.

But I also saw something else: the boat Tara had spoken of. Landon was waving his arms like a crazed windmill, trying to get the attention of whoever was on board. And it appeared that someone must have spotted us, because the boat was headed in our direction.

Jennifer emerged from the hatch, and the four of us stood there, watching the water and the approaching boat in the distance. There was no sign of the megalodon.

"We have to jump in and swim away from the submarine," she said.

"Why can't we just wait here?" I asked. "Maybe that boat will get here before the sub sinks."

Jennifer shook her head. "It's too risky," she said. "We don't have any other choice. If the sub sinks while we're on it, it will create a vacuum in the water that will pull us down with it. The force will be so strong that we won't be able to swim away. We'll be dragged down to the bottom of the lake, right along with the sinking submarine."

"But," Landon protested, "that . . . that *thing* is out there. He could swallow all of us in one bite."

I did *not* want to jump into the lake. Certainly not with that megalodon around. But like Jennifer said: we really didn't have any other choice.

Lake water began pouring in and down the hatch.

"Come on!" Jennifer said. "Everybody in the water! The sub is going to go down fast!" She grabbed my wrist with her left hand, and Tara's hand with her other. Tara grabbed Landon's hand.

"On three," Jennifer said. "One, two . . . three!"

The four of us leapt from the hatch and plunged into the water. Just before we hit the surface, I had a horrifying vision of the megalodon coming up out of the water at that instant, his hungry mouth open, ready to catch all four of us in his razor-sharp teeth. Thankfully, it was only my imagination, and the four of us hit the water without seeing the giant shark.

We went beneath the surface for only a moment, then popped back up.

"Swim away from the sub!" Jennifer said. "It's

starting to go down!"

She had no sooner said those words than the submarine's hatch vanished beneath the surface with a blast of hissing air and loud, gushing, gurgling sounds. I began to swim, and I could actually feel the suction of the water as it tried to pull me down with the sub. It took a lot of effort, but the four of us were able to safely swim out of the dangerous down current.

In the distance, the boat churned toward us. I could see the shadow of a man in the cabin, piloting the craft, and I was certain he had spotted us and was coming to our rescue.

"Keep swimming!" Jennifer shouted. "Keep swimming, and let's all keep together!"

The four of us crawled through the water. Once again, I wished I had my swim trunks on. It was difficult to swim in all of my clothing. I would be able to swim a lot faster without my pants and shirt clinging to my skin. My shoes felt heavy, too, and it was hard to kick my legs.

Then, Landon let out a horrifying shriek.

"Behind us!" he squealed. *"That . . . that thing is coming!"*

I turned, only to see the giant fin in the

distance, cutting through the water like the blade of a knife.

Question was: who was going to get to us first? The boat . . . or the megalodon?

29

Seeing the fin behind us—even though it was some distance away—gave me a tremendous burst of energy. I crawled through the water, curling my arms forward and down and kicking with my legs. My clothing seemed to slow me down even more. Once again, I wished I was wearing my swimming trunks.

Ahead, the boat was still forging toward us. I could still see the dark shadow of the man in the cabin as he came closer. I didn't see anyone else on the boat.

Behind us, the gigantic megalodon was quickly approaching. His fin was larger than ever, towering into the sky, and I knew if we didn't get out of the lake soon, we were going to be nothing more than tasty treats.

The boat slowed as it drew near, and the man emerged from the cabin and rushed to the side of the boat. He was wearing blue jeans, a white T-shirt, a red baseball cap, and dark sunglasses.

"Hurry!" he shouted. "Swim closer, and grab my hand!"

The boat was still a few feet away, but the four of us swam to it and reached up at the same time. We all wanted out of the lake as fast as possible.

Tara was first. The man grabbed her hand and pulled her out of the water. Jennifer was next, then Landon, then me. I was yanked up with such force that I thought the guy was going to take my arm off. No matter. The important thing was that we were out of the water . . . and without a second to spare, too.

We stood on the boat, dripping wet. Although I could see only the fin of the huge shark, I knew that his head was a lot closer. While we watched, the giant fin turned and began circling us, but he kept a good distance . . . for now.

"You saved us!" Landon said to the man.

"This is unbelievable!" the man said. "That was a real, live shark!"

Jennifer shook her head. "Not just any shark," she said. "A megalodon. How it got here, I'm not sure. But we have to get to safety. We're still in danger, even though we're in your boat. That thing could easily capsize us."

The man hustled back to the cabin and took the wheel. "Everybody hang on!" he shouted. "We're getting out of here!"

I grabbed the boat's railing with both hands, just as the engines began to roar and the vessel started to turn. Not far away, the megalodon's fin was now coming toward us, and I was certain that, given the size of the fish, his snout must be close to the boat.

No matter. I was sure the boat was faster than the giant shark. The boat had already started to move, and it would be only a matter of minutes before we arrived safely on shore. Finally, our nightmare was coming to an end.

Suddenly, there was an enormous jolt that shook the entire boat, nearly knocking me overboard. If I hadn't had a good grip on the railing, I would have been sent sailing into the lake. Landon fell to the deck, and Tara was nearly knocked over the railing, too. The man who'd rescued us was knocked backwards in the cabin, where he fell with a grunt and a loud crash.

Then, there was an eerie silence. All we could hear were the waves lapping at the boat, and it took me a moment to realize what had happened.

"That thing bit us!" Landon said as he got to his feet. "He bit the boat!"

I pointed toward the back of the boat. "Not only that," I said, "he chewed off the boat engine! He ripped it right off the back of the boat!"

At the stern, there was a gaping hole where the motor had been. The megalodon had ripped the entire engine from the boat.

The good thing was that the boat wasn't leaking water . . . the bad thing was that the megalodon's fin suddenly popped back up, and the giant shark began circling us again.

"This just gets worse and worse," Tara said. She started to cry, and I felt bad for her.

"We'll make it," I said. "Someone will come to rescue us." Sure, I didn't even believe myself. Not at that moment, anyway. Things were about as bad as they could get.

The man emerged from the cabin, followed by Jennifer. We all were silent as the enormous fin continued circling the boat.

Without a motor, there was no way for us to escape, and with every passing second, the megalodon circled closer, and closer and closer . . . .

30

As the megalodon circled the boat, I saw something that made my spirits leap: the man who'd rescued us had a phone! He had already dialed and was holding it to his ear.

"We have an emergency!" he said, nearly shouting. "We're in Sardis Lake, and there is a giant shark attacking us!"

He paused for a moment, listening. My eyes darted from the man, then to the giant fin in the water, then back to the man again.

"No, this *isn't* a joke!" he said. "We can't believe

it, either. We need help! There really *is* a giant shark attacking us!"

Jennifer shook her head. "He's going to have a hard time convincing anyone that we're being attacked by a megalodon," she said.

Tara spoke. "For our sake, I hope he can," she said. "We really need some help."

"I don't want to be shark bait," Landon said.

The man with the cell phone continued talking, trying to convince the emergency operator that he wasn't joking. Finally, he finished speaking and put the phone in his pocket. During this time, the megalodon's fin sank into the water, and the fish vanished once again. In the distance, we could see a few more boats venturing out onto the lake. None of them, unfortunately, seemed to be heading in our direction.

"I think they're going to send a helicopter," he said. "It took some time to convince him that we really do have an emergency out here."

"How did you know to come and help us?" Jennifer asked the man.

"I was headed out to fish," he replied. "I saw what I thought was a submarine, which made me curious. Never seen a sub in Sardis Lake before.

Anyway, I saw you guys come out the hatch, and it looked like you were in trouble. Then, I saw the fin. Craziest thing I've ever seen in my life!"

"Us, too," I said.

By now, most of the fog had lifted. The sun was rising into a cloudless, blue sky. It would have been a perfect day . . . except, of course, for the fact that there was a hideous beast lurking beneath the surface of the lake.

Jennifer walked over to the cabin and ducked inside. They began talking, but we couldn't hear what they were saying.

"I sure hope that helicopter gets here fast," Tara said. "That thing could attack this boat at any minute."

We nervously looked around the lake, expecting to see the enormous fin rise up out of the water. The only thing we saw were a few other boats, far in the distance.

"Maybe the megalodon will go after someone else," Landon said.

"Let's hope so," I said. "I mean . . . I don't want anyone else to get hurt. But I hope that thing leaves us alone."

"Maybe he got bored," Tara said. We continued

to scan the lake, but we saw no sign of the megalodon.

Soon, we heard a low, deep drone in the distance.

"There it is!" Landon said. "Look!" His arm shot out, and he pointed.

Low in the sky and far away was a dark dot. The sound grew louder and became heavy, steady thumps.

"The helicopter!" Tara exclaimed.

Jennifer and the man emerged from the boat's cabin. We all watched the helicopter as it flew low over the lake. Once again, I was filled with hope that we were going to be rescued. After all we'd been through, our ordeal was over.

Almost. We'd thought the megalodon had gone somewhere else . . . but he was only waiting for another chance at us.

31

Tara, Landon, and I began waving our arms in the air to attract the attention of the helicopter pilot as he approached. It really wasn't necessary, as the chopper pilot had already spotted us. Still, we were excited about being rescued, and it felt like we should do *something*. Landon even jumped up in the air and bounced up and down.

"Finally!" he shouted. "We're getting out of here! We're going to be rescued!"

The helicopter was red and white and had some numbers and letters on the side, but it was going so fast, we couldn't read them. It flew directly over us, and the heavy thumping of its blades was deafening. I could actually feel the sound go through my entire body. Then, the chopper turned and came back around in a wide arc.

And as if on cue, the giant fin of the megalodon appeared in the distance. The helicopter pilot saw it, and I could see him in the cockpit, talking on his radio. He slowed the chopper and headed toward the shark, finally hovering above it in the sky. From his vantage point in the air, I wondered if he was able to see the silhouette of the fish beneath the surface. Regardless, I was sure the pilot was as freaked out as we were!

"Leave the fish alone and come get us," Tara said as if she were speaking to the helicopter pilot.

"Yeah," Landon said. "I want out of this lake. In fact, I'm never going in this lake again. Ever."

The megalodon changed his course and began heading for us. When the helicopter pilot saw this, he guided the aircraft toward our boat. As he drew near, I saw another man inside the helicopter. He was sitting by a door on the side that was open. While we watched, the man pulled out a big basket and dropped it out the door, where it dangled on a short rope.

"Yes!" I said. "We're being rescued! We're getting out of here!"

By now, the helicopter was about one hundred feet from us, a shiny red and white bundle of steel beneath a rich, blue sky.

Suddenly, we heard a voice coming from a loudspeaker in the chopper.

"We're lowering the basket!" a man's voice boomed. "We'll bring you up one at a time! Be sure to buckle yourself in!"

We watched as the large basket lowered from the helicopter. The pilot brought the craft closer and closer.

"Hey," Tara said. "Look." She pointed to the large fin in the water. "He's heading toward the helicopter."

"Fine with me," Landon said. "As long as he doesn't come after us. Besides: there's no way he can get the helicopter. It's too high in the sky."

Landon was right. I didn't think the shark would be able to leap up and get the helicopter.

What it *did* do, however, was something totally unexpected: as it drew closer, the shark suddenly picked up speed. With an enormous lunge upward, the shark's head came up and out of the water . . . and took the entire basket in its mouth! The helicopter jerked madly, and the man near the door almost fell out.

The shark sank back into the water with the basket in its mouth, and with a sudden wave of horror, I realized what was about to happen.

The shark was pulling the helicopter down! It was going to crash into the lake!

32

Watching the scene unfold was worse than any nightmare I'd ever had . . . and I've had some bad ones. I had a nightmare about a monster in the closet and another one about a giant snow monster chasing me. Those weren't half as scary as what I was seeing in Sardis Lake.

We could still see the megalodon's fin and part of his snout. He had the rescue basket in his mouth, which was still connected to the cable. As the fish thrashed about, it was yanking the helicopter.

Then, the megalodon vanished. However, he

still had the rescue basket, and the helicopter was being pulled closer and closer to the water.

"Oh, no!" Tara gasped, and she covered her mouth with her hands.

We could see the helicopter pilot frantically trying to steer the aircraft up and away from the water. It looked like the other guy was trying to get the cable disconnected.

Suddenly, when the helicopter was only a few feet from the surface of the lake, it suddenly rose high into the air. The cable was pulled with it, and I figured the megalodon had let go of the rescue basket.

But that wasn't the case. The cable came all the way out of the water . . . but there was no basket. The end of the cable was chewed and frayed.

"The megalodon bit the cable!" I said, pointing.

"That was a close one," Landon said. "In two more seconds, the helicopter would have been pulled into the lake."

"But how are we going to be rescued?" Tara asked. "Now that the basket is gone, how are we going to get into the helicopter?"

"Maybe we'll have to climb the cable," Landon said.

I shook my head. "No," I said. "That would be too dangerous."

"In case you hadn't noticed," Landon said, "we're in a lot of danger right now. I don't think we could be in any more danger."

Landon was right, of course. Still, I didn't think it would be a good idea to try to climb the cable. It would be too easy to fall. Or, maybe the megalodon would leap out of the water and gobble one of us up, just like he had done with the rescue basket.

The helicopter moved closer to us. Jennifer and the boat captain had been in the cabin, watching through the window. Now, they came out and stood at the bow of the boat, looking up.

The helicopter pilot's voice came over the speaker again. While we watched, the man seated at the side of the helicopter spooled out more cable.

"Tie the cable to your boat!" he said loudly. "We'll pull you to the shore!"

"Great idea!" I said as the boat captain waited for the cable to be lowered. The helicopter hovered above us, and I could feel the wind from the powerful, churning blades. It tossed my hair wildly about and caused the surface of the lake to ripple and foam.

Lower and lower the chopper came, until the cable was within reach. The boat captain grasped it and tied it to a cleat at the front of the boat. A cleat is an anvil-shaped piece of metal used to secure boat lines. We didn't have any on our rowboat, but most bigger boats, like the one we were now in, had several cleats at the bow and stern, and even more along the sides.

When the cable was secure, the man looked toward the chopper and stuck his thumb in the air. Then, he turned toward us.

"Everybody hang on," he said, and he strode to the cabin. "In fact, let's all sit in here, so there's no danger of anyone falling overboard."

That seemed like a good idea. The last thing I wanted to do was fall into the lake when we were about to be rescued!

The helicopter began to move forward, and the cable tightened. I could feel the boat begin to move.

Tara suddenly gasped. "He's coming back!" she shouted. "He's behind us!"

We all turned to see the giant fin appear in the water behind the boat. He was a long ways away, but it looked like he was moving fast.

The helicopter pilot must have seen the shark, too, because he picked up speed. The boat began to churn through the water, leaving a large wake in its path.

Faster, I thought. *We're going to have to go faster if we're going to outrun that thing.*

"He's gaining on us!" Landon shrieked.

The helicopter began to move even faster. The boat thundered across the water, and we all held onto anything we could to keep from bouncing around. It's a good thing we were in the cabin, too, as it would have been too bumpy to remain on deck. One of us would have been tossed overboard, for sure.

But the megalodon was still gaining. Clearly, he could move faster than the helicopter. Oh, I'm sure the helicopter could move much faster than the giant shark. But with a boat in tow, the chopper couldn't reach a high rate of speed.

We were about a half-mile from shore, and I calculated that we would be on land in less than two minutes. I would have been right, too.

But the megalodon was about to prove me wrong. We were about to find out that he was *not* going to let our boat make it to safety.

33

As our boat bounced madly across the surface, the only thing we could do was watch as the giant fin came closer and closer. I knew we were moving as fast as we could, but it wasn't fast enough.

Suddenly, my worst fear came true. Right behind the boat, the megalodon's snout emerged from the water. I could see his angry, dark eyes. His mouth opened wide . . . and with a powerful surge, he lunged forward. His mouth was like a pink and black cave filled with sharp stalagmites and stalactites.

"Everybody get to the front of the boat!" the

captain ordered. "Hurry!"

The five of us scrambled out of the cabin and darted to the bow of the boat. It was hard, too, because the boat was rocking and bouncing as we moved across the surface of the lake.

Suddenly, the mighty jaws of the megalodon were upon us. The shark's mouth was so big that he was able to take the entire back end of the boat into his mouth! He clamped down tightly, and we could hear the sounds of snapping fiberglass, metal, and glass. The boat was brought to a halt, and we all had to hold onto the railing to keep from being tossed out the front of the boat.

Tara was screaming. Landon was shrieking. It was total chaos! The megalodon was chomping at the boat like he was gnawing on a candy bar! Pieces of the boat were coming off and falling into the water.

"We're going to be eaten alive!" Landon screamed. "We're going to be shark food!"

"The cable!" Jennifer shrieked. "It's our only hope! Everyone grab hold of the cable, and don't let go!"

"But it's tied to the boat!" I shouted. However, as soon as I'd said those words, the captain untied the cable.

Meanwhile, the megalodon continued eating away at the boat. By now, we were only a few feet away from his jaws.

"Grab the cable and climb!" the man ordered. I grabbed the cable with both hands and began pulling myself up. Every muscle in my body seemed to ache, but I hardly noticed it. Tara grabbed the cable just below me. Jennifer and Landon were next, followed by the boat captain.

"Go!" the boat captain shouted up to the helicopter.

In the next instant the giant megalodon lunged, and finished off what remained of the boat. If we would have waited one more second, we would have been gulped down like human cupcakes.

The helicopter rose into the sky, and I held onto the cable with all the strength I had. Below us, the megalodon was gnawing angrily at what was left of the boat. Clearly, he was mad that we'd escaped.

"Is everyone all right?" Jennifer shouted. It was hard to hear her over the rushing wind and the thumping blades of the helicopter.

"I am!" Tara said. "But I don't know how long

I'll be able to hang on!"

"We'll be on land in a minute!" the boat captain shouted. "Just don't let go of the cable!"

My worst fear was that the cable would break. Or, maybe Tara wouldn't be able to hang on, and she would accidentally knock me off, too. Then, if the fall into the lake didn't kill us, the megalodon would, for sure.

But I needn't have worried. As we drew closer and closer to land, I could make out docks, boats, and homes. I saw beaches. There was one beach that was larger than the others, and that's where we were headed. The helicopter slowed and lowered, slowly, slowly . . . .

Finally, when we were only a few feet off the ground, the boat captain let go of the cable and dropped to the sand. Jennifer and Landon were next, then Tara, then me. I fell when I hit the ground, and sand stuck to my wet clothing. I didn't care. I was just glad to be off the lake. I was glad to be alive.

Seeing that we were okay, the helicopter rose into the sky and headed out over the lake. As the sound of the whirring blades faded, I could make out other sounds: sirens. The police were on their way.

Probably fire engines, too, along with other emergency response vehicles.

"We made it!" Tara said. "I can't believe we actually made it!"

"I thought we'd never get off the lake alive," Landon said.

"Nobody is going to believe this," I said.

"Oh, yes they will," Jennifer said. "We aren't the only ones who saw that thing. The important thing now is to keep everyone off the lake. No one is safe, as long as that megalodon is in the water."

I wondered what was going to happen to it. Would someone try to capture it? Kill it? I mean, sure, it posed a great danger to anyone in the lake. But it seemed like it would provide a huge amount of scientific information, if it could somehow be kept alive and studied.

We said goodbye to Jennifer, and I told her that I hoped we would see her again.

"Oh, I'll be around," she said. "And stop by my laboratory anytime."

"Let's go home," I said to Tara and Landon. "My parents are going to freak when I tell them what just happened."

"Are we going to be famous?" Landon asked.

"I don't care," Tara replied. "I'm just glad I'm back on land and away from that terrible thing in the lake."

A police car appeared and squealed to a stop in the parking lot of a nearby marina. An ambulance followed.

I shook my head. "I can't believe we made it," I said. "I can't believe this whole thing is over."

Oh, it wasn't *quite* over. We had no idea that the *real* excitement was about to begin.

34

It took us a few minutes to get home, because the beach where the helicopter dropped us off was about a mile from where we lived. Plus, another policeman showed up and wanted to talk to us. He asked us a lot of questions. We told him what had happened, everything we saw. He took down our names and said he might contact us again with more questions.

After he left, we headed home. We walked quickly, taking long strides, chattering nonstop. I tried to brush off the sand that stuck to my wet clothing. All the while, I wondered how I was going to explain all of this to Mom and Dad.

"When I talk to my mom and dad, it would help if you guys were with me," I said to Tara and Landon. "That way, you could back up my story. Otherwise, my parents are going to think I'm just telling a fib."

"We'll go with you," Tara said. "But when this whole thing gets out on the news, they'll *have* to believe you."

"I can't believe how lucky we were," Landon said. "Think about it: we're the only kids in the world that have been attacked by a real, live megalodon!"

"I would have rather it happened to someone else," I said.

"Me, too," Tara agreed. "I didn't think we'd ever set foot on land again."

We could still hear sirens in the distance. I figured the police and fire departments were busy making sure everyone was off of the lake. It would be a tough job, too, because Sardis Lake is so big. How on earth were they going to get everyone off the lake and keep them off? I tried to imagine what it would be like when a police officer told someone to get off of the water . . . because of a shark! In Sardis Lake?!?!

Sure, it *sounded* crazy . . . but we knew better.

We'd seen the thing with our own eyes.

We rounded a corner, and my house came into view. Dad was outside, tinkering with the lawnmower. When he saw me, he got a really puzzled look on his face.

"I thought you went fishing," he said.

"Well," I began, "we did. Sort of."

Dad stop working on the mower and looked at me, then Tara, then Landon. "You guys look like you've been swimming. Did you fall in the lake?"

"Yeah, that too," Landon said.

"Dad," I said, "I don't know how to tell you this, but we were attacked by a giant shark."

"Yeah," Landon said. "A huge one."

"A megalodon," Tara chimed in.

Dad looked at me, then Landon, then Tara. "Okay," he said with a grin. "What's the punch line? I'll bet it's pretty funny."

I shook my head. "I know you're not going to believe us now," I said, "but later, when it's on the news, you'll know the truth. There really is a live megalodon in Sardis Lake."

"Do you hear all those sirens, Mr. Bridgeman?" Tara asked. "Those are the emergency vehicles. I'm sure the police are going around telling everyone to stay off the lake."

At that exact moment, a police car turned the corner and rolled down our street. The light bar on top flashed red and blue, but there was no siren. The vehicle moved slowly.

Then, a voice came over the car's bullhorn. "This is the police," a husky voice boomed. "We have an emergency in Sardis Lake, and we are ordering everyone to stay out of the water until the danger has passed. I repeat . . . ."

The police car rolled by the front of our house, and the police officer's voice continued to boom from the bullhorn.

"See, Dad?" I said. "We aren't kidding. There's a giant shark in the lake. We're lucky to be alive."

Dad looked at me and frowned. "This must be a joke," he said.

The three of us shook our heads. "It's no joke," I said. "Actually, I wish it was. But it's not. This is really, really serious."

"Well, if it's *that* serious, they'll have something on the news," Dad said. He stood up. I could tell he didn't really believe us . . . but he knew something was wrong. "I'll go turn on the television and see what's going on."

"And I'm going to go to Landon and Tara's," I said, "so I can help explain this whole thing to their parents."

Dad strode across the lawn toward our house, and Tara, Landon, and I head toward their home. They only live a few houses away . . . but their parents weren't home. There was a note on the counter that explained they'd gone to run some errands.

"Hey," Tara said. "Let's turn on the TV and see if the news is on."

Oh, the news was on, all right, and we had a front row seat to view all the action that was going on around the lake.

35

The first thing we saw was a news reporter. She was standing on a dock, holding a microphone.

"*. . . no one knows where the giant, prehistoric shark came from,*" she was saying, "*but one thing is for sure: somewhere, here in Sardis Lake, a megalodon is lurking. Police are asking that everyone stay out of the water until the situation is remedied.*"

I laughed. "Just how are they going to 'remedy' the situation?" I said. "There's no way they're going to get that thing out of the lake. We'll never be able to go swimming there again.

175

Well, within a week, I was proven wrong. Scientists and marine biologists, working with Jennifer, came up with a plan to tranquilize the fish. They created a huge ball—nearly the size of a car—and filled it with a special tranquilizer. Then, they dropped it into the water, where it floated just beneath the surface like a giant water balloon. They were hoping the megalodon would find it and eat it. When he did, the ball would break open and release the tranquilizer into his body, causing the beast to fall asleep.

It took a couple of days, but it worked. In fact, scientists were watching from the shore as the megalodon attacked and ate the ball. Within ten minutes, the giant fish was floating sideways on the surface.

Then, the real work began. Using a specially designed net and six helicopters, they scooped up the megalodon and raced south, heading for the ocean. They knew they didn't have a lot of time, as they couldn't keep the shark out of water for very long.

The whole idea was to keep the megalodon alive so they could study him. They planned to release him in a deep, salt-water bayou next to the sea, so he couldn't escape into the ocean.

And everything went as planned . . . until they released the fish in the water. Then, something incredible happened.

36

The megalodon *shrank.*

I heard about it from Tara. It was just after dinner, and all of a sudden there was loud pounding on our front door.

"I'll get it," I told Mom and Dad, and I raced across the living room and opened the door. Tara was standing with her fist in the air, ready to knock again. Her eyes were wide with excitement.

"Did you hear?!?!" she exclaimed.

"Hear what?" I asked. "What's wrong?"

"The megalodon!" she replied. "It shrank! When

they put it in salt water, it got smaller! It's on the news right now!"

Our television was already on, and I switched the station until I found a national news channel.

"They think the fresh water had something to do with the shark getting so big," Tara said. "They think that—"

"Shhh," I said. "They're talking about it right now."

We watched as they replayed footage of the megalodon being lowered into the bayou. At first, it looked like the shark might be dead. When they pulled away the giant net, the fish just rolled sideways, like he was dying.

But then, he started swimming around. Not only that, while we watched, we could see that he was shrinking! He was actually getting smaller, right before our eyes!

"Look!" I said, pointing. "There's Jennifer! She's on television!"

Jennifer was being interviewed, and she was asked to explain what she thought had happened. She told the reporter about her theory that a baby megalodon had been trapped in amber for millions of years, and the fresh water had revived it.

"However," she went on to say, "I believe the fresh water caused a radical change to the fish's metabolism," she said.

"What's a metabolism?" Tara asked.

"Shhh!" I said.

"The fish had a bad reaction to the fresh water," Jennifer continued, "somehow causing it to grow to enormous proportions over a short period of time. When it came in contact with salt water, the process was reversed. That doesn't explain everything, but we hope to learn more in the coming days and weeks."

By then, the police had declared Sardis Lake safe, and people began returning to the water. Not everyone, though. Many people were still afraid there might be another megalodon, lurking in the depths, waiting.

And some people even earned money from the whole thing. Stores began selling 'Sardis Lake Megalodon' T-shirts and hats. There were bumper stickers that read, 'I survived Sardis Lake.' I thought that was pretty smart, taking something that could have been tragic and turning it around to earn money. Somebody was thinking, that's for sure.

After a few weeks of studying the megalodon (in his much smaller form) Jennifer returned to her lab. We rode our bikes to see her once in a while, and she was always happy to see us. Occasionally, we talked about what had happened on the lake . . . but not often. It had been too scary, too real. It was a part of my life that I didn't want to keep reliving over and over and over. In fact, that's why I wrote it all down in book form, so I could be done with it and move on with my life.

School began in the fall, and all our friends asked us about what had happened. So, of course, we had to tell them. They listened in amazement as we told them how I'd first spotted the fin from our dock, all the way up to when the helicopter rescued us and flew us to safety.

One student in my class was new. She was tall, with long, jet-black hair. She came up to me one day while I was walking home from school.

"Hey, you're the kid that was attacked by the megalodon," she said.

"I'm one of them," I replied.

"I'm Tricia Levine," she said. "I'm from Oklahoma. My family just moved here."

"I'm Robbie Bridgeman," I replied.

"Don't worry," she said. "I'm not going to ask you to tell your story to me. I've heard all about it, and you're probably tired of talking about it."

"You're right," I said. "I am."

"But I've got a story that's just as freaky," she said. "I thought you might want to hear it."

"Something that happened to you?" I asked.

Tricia nodded. "Last year, as a matter of fact. It had to do with what we thought was a strange sickness."

"What was it caused by?" I asked.

"This is where it gets freaky," Tricia said with a grin. "You won't believe me if I tell you."

I stopped walking and looked at her. "Try me," I said. "I was attacked by a giant, prehistoric shark over the summer. There's not a lot I won't believe."

"Okay," Tricia replied. "It was caused by cooties."

"What?!?!" I replied. "Cooties?!?! You're out of your mind! Cooties aren't real!"

"Do you want to hear what happened, or don't you?" she replied.

I searched her eyes. Somehow, I could tell she

was being truthful.

Cooties? I thought. *There's no such thing. Cooties are just made up.*

"Okay," I said. "Let's hear it."

Tricia began her story, and told me all about the Oklahoma Outbreak . . . .

Next:

#26: Oklahoma Outbreak

Continue on for a FREE preview!

Monday at school was just like any other day in Tulsa, Oklahoma. The bell rang at exactly eight-thirty. I had exactly two minutes to get to my classroom.

But within those two minutes, something happened that would set the stage for an unbelievable series of events . . . turning an otherwise normal day into what could only be described as a horrifying roller coaster ride of terror.

"Tricia! Hey, Tricia! Wait up!"

When I heard my name being called, I turned. Of course, I'd already recognized the voice. It was Carlos Marcos, a friend I've known since first grade.

The hall was packed with dozens of other chattering, laughing students, scurrying like ants to their classrooms. Carlos was weaving through the hoard, snaking around kids as he made his way toward me. I took a few steps aside so I wouldn't be standing in the middle of the hallway, and leaned against a locker.

Carlos came up to me. He had his backpack slung over his shoulder, and his shoes were untied, like usual. Like usual, I had to remind him to tie them. One of these days he was going to trip, fall, and land square on his face.

"Hey," Carlos said.

"Hey, yourself," I replied, and I pointed to his shoes.

"Oh, yeah," he said, and he kneeled down to tie them. While he worked with the laces, he looked up at me and spoke. "Did you read chapter seven?" he asked. His eyes were wide with excitement.

I nodded. "I'm way past that," I said. "In fact, I'm all the way up to chapter fifteen. The book is really freaky."

"I can't wait for book club tonight," Carlos said, getting to his feet.

"Me, too," I replied. "I can't wait to finish the book. Last night, I read beneath the covers with a flashlight, and my mom and dad never knew it."

Carlos and I are in a book club with ten other students. All of us love to read, and, with the help of Mrs. Candor, the school media specialist, we formed an after school book club. Every month, we choose a book for all of us to read, on our own, and we get together every Monday after school to discuss it. It's a blast. Not only do we read some really cool books, but it's fun to get together with friends to talk about the story we're reading. Mrs. Candor usually brings snacks like cookies or cupcakes, which is cool.

Just then, Tommy Gersky, carrying his blue folder with homework, emerged from the throng of hustling students. He's in our book club, too.

"Hey, guys," he said.

"Hi, Tommy," I replied.

"How's it going?" Carlos asked.

"Cool as butter," Tommy replied with a wink. That's a phrase he always says, and he always winks when he says it. When things were going good, he always said everything was as 'cool as butter.' Which is a little strange, being that butter isn't always cool.

Regardless, they might have been as 'cool as butter' at that moment, but in less than five seconds, 'cool as butter' was going to turn into icy terror . . . and it all started when a girl accidentally bumped into Tommy.

2

Tommy was just about to say something, when he was suddenly knocked forward. He dropped his folder, and papers spilled out all over the floor. He snapped around angrily to see Brianna Carson. She's another person who's part of our book club, too.

She had a shocked look on her face. "I'm so sorry," she said. "I wasn't looking."

"Watch where you're going," Tommy snapped. He rubbed his arms and shoulders like he was brushing something off. "That's how cooties are spread," he said. "I've probably got cooties all over me, now."

"I don't have cooties!" Brianna said. She

sounded hurt.

"That's because you gave them all to me," Tommy taunted, still brushing the imaginary cooties from his arms and shoulders.

"I said I was sorry," Brianna said. She stormed off, vanishing into a sea of other students.

"That wasn't very nice," I said to Tommy.

"Yeah," Carlos agreed.

"Hey, she ran into me," Tommy replied as he knelt down to gather up his papers and folder. "Besides . . . I was only kidding."

"Still, it wasn't very nice," I said.

Tommy was indifferent. "She'll get over it," he replied. "It's not like I punched her, or anything."

Now, Tommy isn't a bad kid, but sometimes, he says things without thinking. I think everyone does, once in a while. But he didn't realize little comments like that can hurt people's feelings.

Regardless, the matter was dropped. Tommy headed to his classroom, Carlos went to his, and I went to mine. We're all in sixth grade, but we all have different classrooms. It would have been fun if all three of us had the same teacher, but we didn't. I had Mr. Billings. He was really nice, but he always gave us way too much homework . . . especially on the weekends.

The day passed like any other. I had lunch with Tommy and Carlos in the cafeteria, and I went to gym class and the library. When the bell rang and classes got out, I was relieved that Mr. Billings hadn't given us any homework at all. It would have been hard, being that I had book club to go to, which usually lasts a couple of hours.

It was three o'clock. Book club started in thirty minutes. Usually, I meet Tommy and Carlos in the hall next to my locker, which is where I found Tommy waiting for me.

"I forgot my book at home," he said, "and they don't have any extra copies in the library."

I shrugged. "It doesn't matter. We won't be doing any reading. We'll just be talking about the book. And Mrs. Candor told me earlier that she brought us chocolate chip cookies!"

"Cool as butter," Tommy said.

Carlos arrived a couple minutes later. His shoes were untied again, and he looked puzzled. Worried, even.

"Something's wrong," he said as he walked up

to us.

"Of course something's wrong," Tommy said. "Your shoes are untied again."

Carlos looked at his feet and knelt down to tie them.

"No," he said, looking up as his fingers worked the laces. "I mean, with Brianna. I just saw her on my way here. She was in the library, and she looked sick."

"What do you mean?" I asked. "Like, she caught a cold or something?"

Carlos finished tying his shoes and stood. He shook his head. "It's worse than that," he said. "I only saw her for a moment. She looked really pale, and there were dark circles around her eyes. And another kid in our book club—Wayne—he looked sick, too. I think they might have the flu. I hope it's not going around."

Carlos was right about one thing: Brianna and Wayne were sick, all right.

But it wasn't the flu.

It wasn't a cold or anything like it. In fact, the illness was caused by something that, up until that moment, I thought had been made-up.

A joke.

But it wasn't.

The illness was real, and so was the cause of it.

Cooties.

We didn't know it at the time, but the dangerous cootie infection had already spread to other students in our school, and there was no stopping it.

The Oklahoma Outbreak had begun.

3

We chatted in the hall for a moment, listening to the sounds of the school emptying: slamming lockers, laughter, talking, shoes scuffing the tile floor, friends calling out to friends. There was an announcement on the school public address system, saying that the Monday afternoon book club would begin in twenty five minutes in the library.

"If Brianna and Wayne are sick," I said, "they'll miss book club."

"That means more chocolate chip cookies for us," Tommy replied, rubbing his belly. "I love chocolate chip cookies."

201

"But, what if they're *really* sick?" I wondered aloud. "What if they have to go to the hospital? That would be awful."

"I don't know where they went," Carlos said, "but I'm sure they won't be at book club. I'll bet they went home. They looked like they crawled out of their own graves."

"Come on," I said. "Let's head for the library. It's early, but the rest of the group is probably waiting. If the rest of the group is there, maybe we can start early."

"And start packing in the cookies," Tommy said, rubbing his belly again. He sniffed the air. "I can almost smell them from here."

We walked down the hall. Carlos carried his backpack, and I carried my books. Tommy's folder was tucked beneath his arm.

"It's weird to be here after school has let out," I said. "It's so quiet."

The halls were empty, and the lights had been turned out. A few teachers had gone home for the day, but a few remained in their classrooms. A few pieces of paper were on the floor, but the custodian, Mr. Jones, would have the place cleaned up soon.

And the only sound we heard was the scuffing of our shoes on the tile floor.

"It's almost spooky," Carlos said. "The school is completely different when no one else is around."

"Hey, that would make a good book," Tommy said. "Someone could write a story about a haunted school."

"Why don't you write it?" I asked.

"Maybe I will," Tommy replied. "I'll write a book about the three of us being in our school with ghosts. I'll make it super-scary, just like the book we're reading right now for book club. I'll make it the scariest book anyone's ever read."

Which, of course, was unlikely. There wasn't a single book written that could be as scary as what was about to happen to us in the library.

ABOUT THE AUTHOR

Johnathan Rand is the author of more than 65 books, with well over 4 million copies in print. Series include **AMERICAN CHILLERS, MICHIGAN CHILLERS, FREDDIE FERNORTNER, FEARLESS FIRST GRADER**, and **THE ADVENTURE CLUB.** He's also co-authored a novel for teens (with Christopher Knight) entitled **PANDEMIA**. When not traveling, Rand lives in northern Michigan with his wife and three dogs. He is also the only author in the world to have a store that sells only his works: **CHILLERMANIA!** is located in Indian River, Michigan. Johnathan Rand is not always at the store, but he has been known to drop by frequently. Find out more at:
www.americanchillers.com

ATTENTION YOUNG AUTHORS!
DON'T MISS

JOHNATHAN RAND'S

AUTHOR QUEST®

THE DEFINITIVE WRITER'S CAMP
FOR SERIOUS YOUNG WRITERS©

If you want to sharpen your writing skills, become a better writer, and have a blast, Johnathan Rand's Author Quest is for you!

Designed exclusively for young writers, Author Quest is 4 days/3 nights of writing courses, instruction, and classes at Camp Ocqueoc, nestled in the secluded wilds of northern lower Michigan. Oh, there are lots of other fun indoor and outdoor activities, too . . . but the main focus of Author Quest is about becoming an even better writer! Instructors include published authors and (of course!) Johnathan Rand. No matter what kind of writing you enjoy: fiction, non-fiction, fantasy, thriller/horror, humor, mystery, history . . . this camp is designed for writers who have this in common: they LOVE to write, and they want to improve their skills!

For complete details and an application, visit:

www.americanchillers.com

Join the Free American Chillers Fan Club!

It's easy to join . . . and best of all, it's FREE!
Find out more today by visiting:

WWW.AMERICANCHILLERS.COM

And don't forget to browse the on-line superstore, where you can order books, hats, shirts, and lots more cool stuff!

Dont Miss:

WRITTEN AND READ ALOUD BY JOHNATHAN RAND!
AVAILABLE ONLY ON COMPACT DISC!

Beware! This special audio CD contains six bone-chilling stories written and read aloud by the master of spooky suspense! American Chillers author Johnathan Rand shares six original tales of terror, including *The People of the Trees, The Mystery of Coyote Lake, Midnight Train, The Phone Call, The House at the End of Gallows Lane,* and the chilling poem, *Dark Night.* Turn out the lights, find a comfortable place, and get ready to enter the strange and bizarre world of **CREEPY CAMPFIRE CHILLERS!**

ONLY 9.99!
over sixty minutes
of audio!

Order online at
www.americanchillers.com
or call toll-free: 1-888-420-4244!

Johnathan Rand travels internationally for school visits and book signings! For booking information, call:

1 (231) 238-0338!

www.americanchillers.com

Also by Johnathan Rand:

GHOST IN THE GRAVEYARD

All AudioCraft books are proudly printed, bound, and manufactured in the United States of America, utilizing American resources, labor, and materials.

USA